WHAT BOOKS PRESS

AN IMPRINT OF

THE GLASS TABLE

COLLECTIVE

LOS ANGELES

REMEMBERING DISMEMBRANCE:

A CRITICAL COMPENDIUM

DANIEL TAKESHI KRAUSE

WHAT
BOOKS
PRESS

LOS ANGELES

Library of Congress Cataloging-in-Publication Data

Names: Krause, Daniel Takeshi, 1977- author.
Title: Remembering dismembrance : a critical compendium / Daniel Takeshi
    Krause.
Description: Los Angeles : What Books Press, [2020] | Includes
    bibliographical references and index. | Summary: "Quirky, cerebral,
    exquisitely tortuous, Daniel Takeshi Krause's first novel, Remembering
    Dismembrance, constructs itself as a second-edition compendium of an
    ongoing critical conversation surrounding a hypothetical novel,
    Dismembrance." -- Provided by publisher.
Identifiers: LCCN 2020027483 | ISBN 9781733378963 (paperback)
Classification: LCC PS3611.R3764 R46 2020 | DDC 813/.6--dc23
LC record available at https://lccn.loc.gov/2020027483

Cover art: Gronk, *untitled*, 2020
Book design by Ash Good, www.ashgood.design

What Books Press
363 South Topanga Canyon Boulevard
Topanga, CA 90290

WHATBOOKSPRESS.COM

REMEMBERING DISMEMBRANCE:

A CRITICAL COMPENDIUM

ABSTRACT

FROM THE OUTSET of the effort to produce the first edition
of Remembering Dismembrance: A Critical Compendium, the prime
motivation has been the continued support of the novel's life in conversation,
among academics and artists, fans and aficionados. The Compendium is a
collection of work that stands in dialogic relation to the novel Dismembrance
and its readers; it serves as an expansion of the text's heteroglossic potential, a
furthering of polyphony and imagination. Successful as the first edition may
be in this regard, over time the Compendium has come to look a bit buttoned
down for our taste, too focused on writing about the novel.

With this second edition, our attention has been paid instead to works that
embody the notion of writing through the novel, whatever that may mean.
Where the contents of the first edition often employ a familiar literary
discourse in order to speak about the novel and its possible meaning(s),
the second edition eschews such questions of "aboutness," offering fewer
answers, opting to evoke the character of the novel instead of its characters,
to explore the power of the novel's language rather than its plot, to be the
dream the novel is having now. In this second edition, ostensibly innocuous
aspects of the novel give rise to new worlds and unfamiliar adventures that
resonate with echoes of the concerns of the source text, their sound gleefully

warped in the wide-open spaces of each new author's imagination. If the pieces included in this second edition move us further from the novel, so be it. Such is the price paid by those who would add to the novel's network of reading but resist the terminal assignment of meaning. If the Compendium's first edition was a carnivalesque imagining in the face of a funhouse mirror, let this second be a stained glass through which to see the novel, blurred but brighter for the freedom its inexactness offers.

"There will be no verification."
—from *Dismembrance: A Strange Encyclopedia*

CONTENTS

LIST OF FIGURES

FOREWORD

"NO RED. RED THIS. Red me you. Drip. Drip drip. Dripping, red.
Red smear red. Black marks red. Black marks red." Thus begins the novel
Dismembrance: A Strange Encyclopedia, a confusing, confused, kaleidoscopic
re-membering of an amputated past that might've been, begun in the visceral,
the viscera, the primordial singularity of pre-personhood on the cusp of
individuation, not yet fully born into language. And with these first sentences,
if indeed they can be called such, the first questions arrive. Who is this red
me you? Where does the red drip red? Why are the black marks red, and why
so insistent? Not much to go on perhaps, but in the *Compendium*, now in
its second edition, these proto-questions are pursued by an array of minds—
scholars, artists, enthusiastic explorers—each of them wandering their own
way through the novel's twisty little passages, stepping as many times as
necessary through the looking glass. With the continued popularity of the
novel pressing it on, the *Compendium* brings to bear a greater number of essays,
a wider variety of artistic output in response to the novel, and previously
unseen excerpts from the novel itself. If, in their exploring, none of the pieces
collected here quite manages to answer the questions with which we begin,
the *Compendium* remains nonetheless an essential companion to any and all
who would like to know just how to get these black marks red. —d.t.k.

PREFACE

"...instead of a field as a vanishing point for the eye, you are in
a reversed depth, which transforms you into a vanishing point..."
—from *Dismembrance: A Strange Encyclopedia*

"REMEMBERING *DISMEMBRANCE*" is a deceptively simple notion.
At first semantic glance, the phrase may appear to imply the variegated hues
of nostalgia bathed in the diffused light of reminiscence—a simple stroll
down memory lane. Or else the solemnity of commemoration, a paean to
the deceased, the tiny constellating fires of Obon illuminating a path back
home. In either sense the sound of the words rings clear, but neither term of
the phrase, examined individually, acquiesces quite so simply. The shortcut
to meaning quickly becomes a short circuit. The errand on which we embark
resists the familiar security of purpose and fulfillment, question and answer,
beginning and end.

REMEMBERING
To remember. In common usage the verb suggests retention or recall, a
recording, a neural trace possessing some identity with the earlier events and
experiences that constitute its origins, kept in this container we call brain,
memories these discrete nouns, static objects we carry deep in our pockets as
we walk forward through what we call linear time. Though memories have
long been known to lose definition and thereby fidelity to the experiences they
are alleged to represent, they are casually accepted as essentially unchanging
copies written into blank space, their erosion over time on the order of the

yellowing of a newspaper, the slow fade of a photograph. In this analogy, remembering is an act of preservation, a sort of rehabilitation, blowing off the dust. The faded memory can be resuscitated; accuracy can be maintained or reclaimed. We study our memories lest we lose sight of what we have done, what has been done to us, who we have known, who we have been and thus who we are. In this conception, eyewitness testimony is admissible; remembering is a reliable way of knowing; we trust our memories to tell us the truth.

But what current and ongoing research increasingly suggests about memory is something teleologically different. As we continue to learn about the material biology of memory, our understanding of remembering as a process grows inextricable from a conception of memory as revision. The case is made by that most literary of organs the hippocampus—named for its uncanny likeness to a seahorse (from the Greek *hippos* meaning "horse" and *kampos* meaning "sea monster")—where new information is encoded as memory, where events become facts, where memories episodic grow semantic, the room to which the memories we carry with us are called back anytime we want them, and often enough when we don't. When a dog at the park reminds you of your childhood pet, or salty air of sunburned summers on the coast, or a song of the last time you saw her, the hippocampus is where we sit to read our own stories. And as each memory is read in this way, in this room, is remembered, it is seen anew and interleaved again, amongst the totality of your memories, adjusting both the content of the particular page and the configuration of the entire network. In this way memory functions not as a vault of sacred documents read with white gloves but as the messy desk of the reader, writer, editor, librarian, storyteller. Memory is an always already evolving narrative continually revised at the occasion and site of its own (re)creation.

And if this is the process we go through each time we remember a trip to the zoo or a broken bone or a Tuesday from last week, what challenge is there in imagining a number of permutations beyond which a memory might be unrecognizable to its own earlier selves? This is not a game of Operator, in which the message is simply corrupted by static in the signal or inattention. Rather this is a process by which the very attention we pay to our memories rewrites them. How many times can you remember your mother's face before you will have forgotten it completely? We are reminded that a record's groove consists of empty space, implying twisted bits of wax and the stylus that raised them, confirming their absence, turning in circles on a slow journey inward, which is to say, nowhere. Remembering, it seems, is an act of forgetting. Or more to the point, to remember and to forget are not in fact binary opposites in a zero sum game. Consider the following:

dismember (v)—1: to cut off or disjoin the limbs, members, or parts of 2: to break up or tear into pieces

revise (v)—1: to look over again in order to correct or improve <revise a manuscript> 2 a: to make a new, amended, improved, or up-to-date version of <revise a dictionary> b: to provide with a new taxonomic arrangement <revising the sempervirens>

remember (v)—1: to rejoin parts, reassemble

And if this be not yet enough to convince you of the complicated nature of that simple notion with which we began, then the last thing we'll add before we continue is a reminder that as mammals, each of us has been apportioned not one sea monster but two, one for each side of our brains, and you know how differently those two see things.

THE NOVEL

And what of the artifact of our remembering, the kairotic occasion of this collection, the novel through which this compendium professes to be? Though it is widely agreed that the novel *Dismembrance* was first collected as a bound codex in 2007 by Tokyo Kitchen Press (commonly referred to as the TKP edition), those familiar with the novel know that *Dismembrance* existed before then in pieces and in places outside the covers of what we commonly call a "book" and has since been collected and continued in several new editions, iterations, and evolutions, each clamoring not only for attention but also authority and that elusive adjective—definitive—even as the novel's presence has continued to grow beyond the borders that have been foisted upon it, manifesting in the landscape that surrounds it and the readers who help to carry it there.

From its earliest (recorded) beginnings just before the turn of the millennium as a series of fragments in the online forum now widely known as The Archive, to the kaleidoscope of interpretations, editions, and additions available today, *Dismembrance* has always been a testament to the diffuse nature of authorship. Roland Barthes says it well when he holds up *Dismembrance* as evidence of a movement toward what he calls the "writerly text":

> ...the networks are many and interact, without any one of them being able to surpass the rest; this text is a galaxy of signifiers, not a structure of signifieds; it has no beginning; it is reversible; we gain access to it by several entrances, none of which can be authoritatively declared to be the main one; the codes it mobilizes extend as far as the eye can reach, they are indeterminable...; the systems of meaning can take over this absolutely plural text, but their number is never closed, based as it is on the infinity of language. (*S/Z* 5)

In the context of Barthes' apt description of the novel, the public's engagement with *Dismembrance* appears nothing less than absolutely appropriate.[1] But while the public debate continues between those who hold up the novel as the progenitor of its readers' uniquely zealous engagement and those who argue instead that the reading public's passionately generative contact with the novel is in fact the catalytic phenomenon responsible for the collective (and collected) image of the novel we attempt to share among us, what is undeniable at this point in the novel's life is that it exists beyond the printed page, has infiltrated the world to which we assign the label "real" and therefore separate from the novel, has blurred the line we imagine that allows us to step not only into but also out of that thing we call fiction. The Carrollian membrane of (non)sense has grown permeable, been passed, and passed again. This truth is borne out not only in the jostling amongst differing editions of the novel but also in the still proliferating

---

[1] For those interested in a more thorough treatment of the novel's readership, the editors recommend Thomas Vander Wal's *Reading Dismembrance: Taxonomy of An Audience*, which lays out the now familiar breakdown of the novel's reading audience into the categories of readers, compilers/hoarders, editors, and authors, along the way discussing the nuances of each group's reading in terms of consumption, manipulation, and production.

series of adaptations to other media, in the enthusiastically apocryphal writings still appearing online and elsewhere that imagine themselves into the empty spaces the novel creates, in the contentiously varied response of many members of the academic community, and ultimately in the novel's continuing presence in popular culture.

All of which is to say that *Dismembrance* is no simple signifier. It does not point directly to any one object. Similarly, one cannot point (perhaps to a copy of the TKP edition) and say, "there it is." The gesture is insufficient, encompassing the novel not so easy. And so our initial notion of "Remembering *Dismembrance*" is difficult on two counts and the job of this compendium is revealed to be more complicated than we might have imagined.

IN SEARCH OF ARTEMIS

And so we set out in search of a novel that only grows more elusive in response to our efforts to remember. Believing ourselves Artemis, goddess of the hunt, we aim our arrows into the brush hoping to preserve the novel, not knowing that we are the prey, chased by our own hounds and torn to pieces once we've spied Artemis at her ease and failed to avert our eyes. In contact with the novel we are the hunted, our remembering not an enterprise in literary commemoration, but an effort to reconstruct a sundered self. In drawing closer to the text we pursue our own dissolution and in the end find that the thing in need of re-membering is none other than the person we thought we were before we began, who is, of course, irretrievable. —t.k.p.

ACKNOWLEDGMENTS

SINCE THE PUBLICATION of the Compendium's first edition in 2011, *Dismembrance* has continued to gather attention and spur conversation. Opinions are as diverse as ever. Disparate readings arrive with regularity. Each new engagement with the novel opens new possibilities of meaning, with seemingly every reader and writer who takes the time to respond arranging the available textual clues into new patterns, finding new notions of just what has happened. At the same time, the contradictory and multiple nature of the source text, as well as the continuing emergence of new and disputed fragments, has thus far fairly well precluded the possibility of any particular reading of the novel gaining true ascendancy. In short, the novel continues its becoming with no one yet in a position to bring the conversation to conclusion or stasis.

Onto unsteady ground then, the Compendium takes a second step. While some entries from the first edition remain, others we have opted to omit as the conversation has steered elsewhere in the intervening years. Still others have been elided not due to a lack of traction but rather its opposite. Many of these have gone on to elicit responses of their own generating entirely new nodes of inquiry, as in the case of the oft-discussed West End Fragment. First published in the Compendium's inaugural edition, the West End Fragment has since inspired a stage adaptation manifesting the text in the form of five discrete characters debating the likelihood of any of them being the result of a truly native memory. The stage play has in turn led to "Venice Beach," the film adaptation with which so many are now familiar, thanks in part to the mainstream distribution and marketing the film earned for itself with a buzzy turn on the festival circuit.

Other notable omissions from the first edition include Paul Harris' *Dismembrance: A User's Manual*, an essay that has spent the years since the first edition's publication living in a steady stream of annotated editions expanding, negating, or otherwise revising Harris' initial argument; Sidney Hamet's "Remembering (in) *Dismembrance*: Neural (Re)consolidation as Textual Revision," a compelling analysis of three of the novel's most echoed passages that has now been anthologized often enough to render its inclusion here unnecessary; *Centering Dismembrance*, an unattributed character sketch detailing the history of the Archivist and consisting solely of lines culled from the novel, complete with citations describing methodology and making the case for its own veracity, but most well-known for including its own rebuttal in a series of annotations to its citations; "Consolidation and reconsolidation: Two lives of memories?" from Dr. Katherine Keane of Boston University's Eichenbaum Laboratory of Cognitive Neurobiology and Literature, which has since gone on to publication in the scientific journal *Synapse* and a well-received keynote presentation at the ninth annual International Symposium in Science and Literature; Brian Richardson's "A Poetics of Memory: Narrating Dismembrance, Unnaturally" since released in an extended version from Ohio State University Press; and "A Life Still Remembered: A Still Life," a triptych in oil on canvas of disputed provenance which serves as the cover art for both the TKP codex and the Compendium's first edition and has since found new life in a hauntingly beautiful work by Canadian performance artist Lia Pas, "She Opened," a monologue delivered as the artist tears an impossibly long red sheet in two, enacting the novel's predicament in the slow movement of the artist and her increasing entanglement—the winding sheet becomes a binding sheet and Pas completes the piece wrapped tightly in the shreds of her material. On the subject of her performance as novelistic adaptation Pas says that, "one ought to think of it as a kinetic metaphor, a corporeal translation of the text," a sentiment clearly internalized by east coast American performance artist Ervin Israel in his off-Broadway one-man show adapting Pas' work, entitled "How to Throw."

As some pieces have stepped aside, others have stepped forward to take their places. In its second edition the *Compendium* is bolstered by the addition of new insight and novel approaches. Notable among these are an introduction to the new edition from acclaimed novelist and first-time reader David Foster Wallace, a series of annotations from venerated poet and critic Paul Chowder, and—in a particular stroke of good fortune for Tokyo Kitchen Press—a modest selection of pieces from Castor P. Rosenthal's beloved collection *Watches from Nagasaki*. In an effort to more thoroughly represent the scope of the novel's existence, also included are excerpts from the novel as collected in the TKP edition, passages generated by the most passionately active segments of the novel's fan base, and disputed fragments of uncertain origin which have nonetheless captured the imagination and consternation of readers and offered new avenues of entry into the questions the novel asks. The editors and publisher of this new edition gratefully acknowledge the volume's new contributors as well as the permission granted by Hairstreak Butterfly Review, the Halophyte Collective, Dream Pop Press, and by the Banff Center for Arts and Creativity to reproduce previously published or performed material.

ACKNOWLEDGMENTS

A NO. A now. An ow. A ledge. An edge. Ack. C?

REMEMBERING
DISMEMBRANCE

INTRODUCTION TO THE NEW EDITION

A Supposedly Fun Book I'll Never Read Again
by[1] David Foster Wallace

I.

Right now I'm sitting in an extremely full coffee shop in an airport, killing
the four hours between when I finally managed to put down *Dismembrance*
and when my flight leaves by trying to summon up the hypnotic sensuous
collage of all the stuff I've seen and heard and done as a result of the readerly
assignment just ended.

I have seen sucrose beaches and water a very bright blue. I have seen an
octopus in ink, arms flared all across the back of a man from head to
buttocks. I have smelled what old age smells like trapped in the dingy
corners of empty-shelved pawnshops. I have watched upscale Americans
slither through row upon row of orphaned, abandoned, and commercially
viable infants connected to semi-permanent electrodes in the nurseries of
someone's apparent nightmares.

I have (very briefly) joined a meeting of Amnesiacs Anonymous. No one talks.

---

[1] As Mr. Wallace was unavailable at time of press, the editors have taken the liberty of writing
the following introduction to the new edition into a substrate consisting of an essay by the
author himself.

I've got to say I feel like there's been a kind of lack of transparency in effect on this assignment. The editors of the *Compendium* keep saying not to fret. They are sort of disingenuous, I believe, these editors. They say all they want is a sort of really big experiential postcard - go, read the book, come back, say what you've seen. Go? Come back? In the mail, I receive this novel, author's name absent. Go, they say. Read the book. Come back, they say. Author's name absent.

I have seen a lot of really big white spaces. I have seen tanks of little fish with fins that glow. I have seen those same fish snatched from those same tanks flayed on rice, still glowing. I have seen the discarded pieces of faceless mannequins overflowing from grey garbage cans in the hidden back hallways of an upscale Los Angeles shopping mall. (The low lighting in the restaurant let the illuminated cheeks of its patrons glow a reddish orange like low-powered fireflies tumbling in place before flitting out after a final swallow.) I have seen the deserted coasts of nameless islands. I have seen 147 homeless men sleeping in and around the Watts Towers. I now know the difference between pawning and remembering and what it is when a junkie "melts." I have heard the rhythm of a Venice Beach drum circle and eaten beluga caviar and watched myself (not me) dressed in the ragged remains of my own clothes projectile vomiting inside a glass elevator. I have danced to the popular music of the day in years before I was born.

I have absorbed the basics of mahjong while waiting for a trace, seen a man in a torn tuxedo pawn his last memory, learned how to secure a pregnant silicon chip to various parts of my scalp, and lost at chess to a ninety-year-old woman. (Actually, it was more like I *smelled* 147 homeless men sleeping in and around the Watts Towers.)

I have dickered over trinkets with malnourished children who don't remember their own names. I now know every conceivable rationale and excuse for somebody choosing to give herself away in return for the chance to be somebody else for less than ten minutes.

I now understand the questions, "Have you seen Mindy?" and, "Do you know Brian?"

I now know how it feels to float in zero gravity.[2] I have, in dark moods, viewed and logged every type of cancerous growth, immunodeficiency, catastrophic injury, inoperable tumor, cardiac event, and unexplained illness that anyone has ever wanted to forget. I have seen naked many people whom I have never actually seen. I have felt as bleak as I've felt since puberty, and have filled almost three Mead notebooks trying to figure out whether it was Them or Just Me. I have acquired and nurtured a potentially lifelong grudge against an author whose name I don't know,[3] and an almost reverent respect for The Archivist.

II.

More specifically: From 11-18 March 1995 I, voluntarily and for no pay, underwent a seven-night effort to read this book from Tokyo Kitchen Press,[4] the only edition—among at least thirty-five disputed versions and repositories of fragments now in the scrum for validity amongst the reading public—that currently maintains a mostly recognized claim of definitive status.[5] The novel is, from what I now understand of it, absolutely top-hole. The prose is superb, the structure impeccably deranged and disarranged, the protagonist organized and erased down to the tiniest detail. The pages so clean and so white they looked boiled behind the black marks I read. The world built varies between an off-putting uncanny valley effect and the equally strange fictitious reality of the simulacra. It is an engrossing read.

---

[2] Though I never did get clear on just who it was I got that memory from.

[3] Somewhere this author seems to have gotten the impression that the over-precious reclusivity which precludes me from using a gendered pronoun here is an important statement on the nature of text. Mildly interesting perhaps, and indicative of someone who is at least semi-literate and has read some Barthes, but frustrating in the face of multiple and extended efforts to locate the single shred of hard evidence of this person's existence which might put my mind at ease w/r/t the origin of this text. I wish this person ill.

[4] Tokyo Kitchen Press, being a publisher of the novel, was of course one of the first places I looked for information that might lead to the novel's author. The website for said publisher, being in possession of only one bit of contact information (an email address), has yet to respond to repeated missives asking after the identity of the author. You are welcome to try your hand at it.

[5] Most prominent among the other editions and incarnations of the novel vying for varying degrees of legitimacy are the FC2 edition, written entirely as a lipogram lacking the letter

All of which is not necessarily to say that I think this book is "good." It's not even so much a good time. It's more like a feeling. It quickly becomes clear that one of the big jobs of any reader of this novel is to keep reassuring oneself that everybody else who read it is wrong, that it is in fact a blind[6] of relaxation and stimulation, a stressless indulgence and frantic tourism, that special mix of distance and possession that's marketed to the reading public under configurations of the phrase "to forget oneself." Obviously, this verb positively infects the text.

III.

This one incident made the Chicago news. Some weeks before I underwent my own reading of *Dismembrance*, a Buddhist monk did a Superman off a third-floor balcony clutching a copy of the novel—a suicide. The news version was that it had been an unhappy meditative divination thing, a life's

---

"i"; the Coffee House Press edition, which most closely approximates the TKP edition in tone but is written from the perspective of the protagonist's journal; there is also, allegedly, a screenplay adaptation of the novel in progress from writer Shane Carruth, though this version has yet to be verified as Carruth has yet to let anyone see it, claiming that while the screenplay is complete he has yet to "put it into words." There is also a graphic novel edition, possibly by the famed and famously cranky author Alan Moore, though in response to the oft-repeated question he adamantly denies authorship, referring to it as "utter crap." The most widely read incarnation after the TKP would certainly have to be the flotsam (and that is meant in the most flattering possible sense of the word) found in the online fan fiction forum started late in the spring of 1999, which originally appeared as "Shadow of The Waxwing," but since the first appearance of the much discussed and oft rewritten West End Fragment has taken instead to referring to itself simply as The Archive. And most polarizing among the editions having gained the critical mass of readership necessary to have an audible voice in the ongoing conversation surrounding the fraught existence of the novel is the Argentinian edition, which consists in fact of a verbatim reproduction of the text of Cervantes' Don Quixote.

[6] This ostensible typo appears to have meant to be the word "blend" rather than the word "blind." This reminds you of the time you fell asleep as a passenger on a long road trip. You awoke and opened your eyes. You felt the road humming beneath you, but you saw only grey fog. Not grey fog outside the car, through the window, but grey fog as if your head were dipped in a bowl of dry ice. You rubbed your eyes. You rubbed them again. You stretched them wide open. You rubbed them again. Still you saw nothing. You began to panic. This is when you felt the pain at the back of your neck and lifted your head off the headrest behind you to look at the world outside your window rather than the grey cloth ceiling of the car.

vow gone bad, etc. I think part of it was something else, something there's no way a real news story could cover.

There is something about a massive novel like *Dismembrance* that's unbearably sad. Like most unbearably sad things, it seems incredibly elusive and complex in its causes and simple in its effect; inside *Dismembrance*—especially at night, when all the day's details and now and here have reached their nadir—I feel despair. The word's overused and banalized now, *despair*, but it's a serious word, and I'm using it seriously. For me it denotes a simple admixture—a weird yearning for death combined with a crushing sense of everything I won't know, can't know, will never remember, or never did, that presents as a fear of death. It's maybe close to what people call dread or angst. But it's not these things, quite. It's more like wanting to die in order to escape the unbearable feeling of becoming aware that I don't remember who I was, don't know who I am, and am going without any doubt at all to die. It's wanting to stop reading.

I predict that this'll get cut by the editors of the *Compendium*, but

7

This marrow-level dread of the oceanic I've never felt before, the feeling of the sea as primordial *nada*, bottomless, unknowable, irrevocably unrecoverable darkness inhabited by cackling tooth-studded things floating eternally beneath a sloshing slate left always blank. This is what *Dismembrance* has given me.

Most of the memories to be found throughout the novel are in various stages of disintegration. And the novel itself (which I found to be fragile as *hell*, like

---

[7] I'm doing this from memory. I don't need the book.

5

nose-falling-off-in-your-syphilitic-hands, its patterns so loosely assembled that it's often like staring at a windy sky full of clouds) turns out to be basically one enormous engine of decay. Tracing corrodes identity with amazing speed— rusts it, exfoliates personality, strips vanity, dulls shine, spreads and makes space between joints with wedges of otherness and fills them with a vague ubiquitous unctuous snot until someone, it might be you, but you can't be sure, yells out Jenga! We saw some real horrors in this book, locals dipped in a mixture of regret and don't-give-a-shit, scabbed with the mind's efforts to heal, ravaged by what they float in.

Not so the protagonist. The story's arc is clearly meant to represent the triumph of identity over the primal decay-action of the novel. The protagonist seems to have a whole battalion of wiry little memories who run around the novel scanning for decay to overcome, arriving always with a roller and a bucket of faces, places, and sensory details. Page after page I read as one or another of these memory-shaped things gave an entire paragraph a fresh coat of paint and walked away with a nod.

Here's the thing. A novel is, for some, a respite from unpleasantness, or at least from the sort that can leave a lasting and tangible trace of itself after a book is closed, and since consciousness of death and decay are unpleasant, it may seem weird that this *Strange Encyclopedia*'s ultimate fantasy involves such primordial decay. But along with and by the protagonist we are enabled in the construction of various fantasies of triumph over just this particular sort of death and decay. One way to "triumph" is via the rigors of self-assertion; and the protagonist's obsessive attempts at upkeep of order are an unsubtle analogue to the traditional accoutrements of narrative: plot, chronology, character, cause and effect, meaning, etc.

There's another way out, too, w/r/t the slippery slope of tracing and the novel. Not upkeep but explosion. Not a tight grip but a letting go. The novel's constant flitting from moment to (not necessarily *next*) moment, the excitement, the stimulation of the transhuman. It makes you feel vibrant, alive. It makes your existence seem non-contingent upon individuality.[8] The letting go promises not an escape so much as transcendence: "Sharing a laugh with yourself,[9] in the lounge of the 'shop, you glance at your face in the mirror and notice it's almost familiar…When the curtain comes down on that last shred of self,[10] you splay your hands and your thoughts turn to, 'Who now?'" (247).

Beckett this isn't, but Dismembrance is nevertheless an extremely powerful and ingenious posthuman argument for a transhuman entity. Put another way, behind the various received narratives that the protagonist attempts to imprint over the essential lack at the center of the novel[11] is a disembodied substance that is contained in the high received from each trace, from every thing remembered. This thing that each junkie knowingly or unknowingly chases (can we simply agree to call it love?) is glimpsed in each trace, a representation of a thing that only means itself. But if all these nameless, past-less Doctor Frankensteins chasing mythology sound to you like so much new age (or old age) hooey, then consider instead the (possibly) last scene in the novel, of The Archive Up In Flames:

> "A burning, up into the sky. And now there will be nothing to which
> the record can be compared. A spectacle, a blackout made from many
> glints of light. A grotesquery of invisible crashing. The evacuation
> complete: The Archivist, me. It's all theater now. ~~There will be no~~
> ~~verification~~. This, the rainbow's end.
>
> The burning looked like other burning. The flames danced red, yellow,
> orange, blue or green, white at its most intense. But what burned

---

[8] The novel's got literally hundreds of time stamps throughout, attached to the protagonist's journal entries and notes or to various artifacts collected—receipts, news articles, bills, emails, envelopes, letters—each one like a red dot on a map to say YOU ARE HERE. It doesn't take long to figure out that the unverifiably jumbled order of said time stamps makes each date a location without context. A journal entry marked for "Tuesday" followed by an entry marked "Sunday" is less for orientation than for some weird kind of muted reassurance that time is out there, somewhere.

[9] Always constant references to "self" in the text; part of this transcendence of death is in the relentless effort to grasp, quantify, define, repeating the word until it loses its wordness and is released into the air as only sound.

[10] See?

[11]

was only containers. Inside containers. Memories don't. There are no ashes to consume, to sit dry in the mouth. They are nothing, and I am obsolete. Will spin only fictions, or if I don't, won't know.

'You can't be rebuilt,' he said.

He said, 'You can't be rebuilt.'

I asked,

And he said, 'It can't be rebuilt.'

And, 'Yes, I can,' I said. It wasn't true.

The heat was tremendous." (759)

IV.

Seductive patter in the world of *Dismembrance* ranges from lighthearted to skin-crawl-inducing, but none of the glossy quarter sheets handed out in Vegas or the passels of ragged children hawking empty memories and animal dreams explains what any reader ought to know before entering this strange encyclopedia.

For all the promises of forgetting, and yes you will forget, it is in fact the thing you can't help knowing and remembering[12] that makes the novel dangerous. There's something crucially key about *Dismembrance* in evidence here: being handled by a text that clearly knows you and feeling that you know yourself only insofar as you read yourself in the pages of the book in your hands. I find myself going farther and farther away inside my head, sort of creatively visualizing a kind of epiphanic moment, pulling mentally back, seeing the protagonist and its reader and its readership and the whole novel itself with the eyes of someone already aboard, with a momentum pulling the moon back

---

[12] Arthur Caplan's Op Ed for MIT Technology Review of June 18, 2013 "Deleting Memories" notwithstanding.

through a skein of clouds, hearing the muffled music and laughter of a million voices throb in the hiss of its receding wake and seeing, from the perspective of the protagonist, good old *Dismembrance* complexly aglow, lit up from within, imperial, impartial, palatial . . . yes, this: like a palace: it would look like a kind of floating palace, majestic and terrible, to any poor soul out here on the ocean at night, alone in the novel, or not even in the novel but simply and terribly floating, a man overboard, treading words, out of sight of all land. This deep and creative visual trance—the novel's true and accidental (sinister?) gift to me—lasted all through the past week, which period I spent entirely in its pages, looking out from within, feeling maybe a little bit glassy-eyed but mostly good—good to be reading and good soon to be done, good that I was surviving (in a way) being remembered to death (in a way)—and so I stayed in the novel. And even though the tranced stasis caused me to miss my grip on the shore from which I embarked and the docking we expect at the end of such a trip, the subsequent choice to get on this plane, to forego reentry into the demands of landlocked "real-world life" wasn't nearly as bad as a week of Absolutely Nothing (or Everything) had led me to fear. —D.F.W.

LETTERS

EVERY NOVEL exists as a conversation, some more lively and enduring than others. *Dismembrance* is one conversation that has already in its young life displayed a distinct inclination for propagation. Were it not for its power to incite response, the first edition of the *Compendium* would never have come to be and we here at Tokyo Kitchen Press would have remained, viz a viz *Dismembrance*, quietly in the role to which editors so often are restricted, that of the silent hand. But *Dismembrance*, for all its empty spaces, does indeed abhor a vacuum, and in the birth of the *Compendium* we the editors of Tokyo Kitchen Press found our opportunity to play a more active role.

Since the publication of the first edition of the *Compendium* the conversation that affects and infects *Dismembrance* has only grown louder and more cacophonous. At the same time the release of the *Compendium* has increased our visibility beyond what it was when we acted merely as purveyors of the source text. More and more it seems we have become a locus for those to whom no other membrane of access is available. The volume and range of the letters we have received from enthusiastically engaged readers since the *Compendium*'s first edition has been a wonderful and rewarding surprise and this epistolary eruption has brought to our attention a new opportunity to populate the novel further and to share the platform we have built.

The dry humor of readers has so impressed the editors that we have chosen to include in this second edition a sampling of the ongoing correspondence, the collected presentation of which we consider fitting tribute to the novel and to the prodigious imaginings and deep investment of those who find themselves inside it. —tkp

DEAR TOKYO KITCHEN PRESS,

As I write this letter, my copy of *Dismembrance* is watching me from the far corner of my desk. I know it's not animate, but I believe it sees me more clearly than I see it. Its straight edges are worn away. Its covers and pages blossom around it in creased and breaking curls. It's lost its knack for closing.

When I first started reading *Dismembrance* I found it bewildering, if not quite inscrutable. The dilapidated state of the novel now (I mean this particular copy of this particular novel that is peering at me at this very moment, nothing larger or more abstract than that) reminds me just how long it's been. And still I don't know that I've got any of it any more figured than when I started. I've read cover to cover and back again. I've pored over sections of the novel. I've found auxiliary materials of all sorts in an attempt to squeeze meaning from the flashes of coherence I've managed to see in its pages. I've set to work on this book with enthusiastic purpose that's given way to weary frustration that's given way to indignant rededication that has, at last, stepped aside to reveal fearful resignation and a desire for self-preservation.

I've read *Dismembrance* and I don't know what I've read. There's someone in this book, someone I feel looking out at me from inside its pages as I'm looking in from out. But this someone, this someone who wanders the pages of the novel in search of an exit while I search for an entrance, I don't know who this person is. I don't know how this person came to be, who is in the novel but not the novel. And I don't know why this someone struggles to leave its place of existence. Is it even possible?

I can't help asking these questions of the book, seeking answers that might let me finally put the blasted thing down. I must be finished with this book, but each day it holds me more tightly. I've tried to leave it alone. Believe me; I've tried. I've tried to read other books, different books, books with characters that have features, traits, histories, books with events presented in some sort of an order, books in which cause precedes effect and effect flows understandably from cause. They sit lifeless in my hands. I can feel *Dismembrance* shaking its head at my naiveté.

In *Dismembrance* I find abstruse unplumbed depths, echoes of traumas I can't name, reflections of memories lacking the requisite detail to take definite shape that blur into ominous blotches and blank spaces, and voices I don't recognize even after I notice them coming from my own mouth. What sort of novel is this? It speaks to me as if I'm familiar to it. Have we met before?

Its early entries were less perplexing. Its confusion was understandable, with the unfamiliar setting of its beginning, surrounded by objects holding the heft of use and of life but revealing nothing more than their surfaces. But the pieces fail to come together. The timing's all wrong! Where is resolution? By the end of the book this narrator, if it's really the same one we started with, seems not to have lost hope of solving its own mysteries but has certainly lost sight of the questions it set out to ask and answer. There are too many voices to keep straight. Why all these memories of empty islands and vast seas? Why so many broken bodies? And where do they all go? Maybe I'm asking the wrong questions, but I haven't got any better.

Tracing, it's fictional, no? So a hypothetical must be harmless. Say the novel went on, goes on, fails to stop. How long might it be before the technology grows? How long could it be before the slow dismantling of individuality gives way to the wholesale up and download of consciousness? Maybe that's too dramatic. Maybe it'd never happen that way, all at once. It'd make time too angular I suppose. Maybe instead it's just that the process goes on so slowly that nobody notices until everything's already too mixed up. If that were the case, hypothetically speaking, at what point would we notice that anything was amiss?

I went for a walk in the park, that one just down the way and around to the west from here. I carried my copy of *Dismembrance* under my arm, obviously. I pressed it tight against my ribs to keep any more of it from getting out. The park was crowded. The weather was fine. It might've been the weekend. The only bench with space to sit sat a few feet from some structures standing in sand and crawling with children swinging and jumping and sliding and falling and spinning in indistinct incessant circles. So much activity and no discernible progress, unless perhaps I heard the hum of young brains building synapses, a hive of honeybees hard at work. I must've sat a long while. Next

I noticed the dwindling hive as mothers and fathers and nannies and uncles and cousins began picking the bees off one by one, strapping them squirming into seats with wheels or packs on backs or fronts until finally the structures stood in quiet sand catching their breath. And then mine caught in my throat. Where was my son? The playground was empty. I jumped and ran around and through the jungle gym, looked up and under metal slides, swung round and doubled back. I lifted my hands, large as I could make them, to my mouth, ready to call his name, hoping to approximate the sound of authority that might cover the panic lumping my throat. I drew in a deep, useless breath. I couldn't call for him. I couldn't remember his name. I couldn't remember his name because he hadn't one. I have no son, never did have. We stopped trying after three miscarriages, two stillbirths, and one (merciful) elective abortion.

It was only when I went back to my bench to pick up my forgotten book that I realized I'd held it under my arm all the while.

I must leave this book. Or I must make it leave me be and take with it these memories I don't understand. I've heard the rumors of a new edition of the *Compendium*. I never heard of the first, but I write now to beg that you do release this next edition, if that's what it is, and sooner than later. I only want to know who this person is at the center of *Dismembrance*. I need to know. My copy of the novel is still watching me now. Was it there all along? Wasn't I sitting in a different corner four pages ago? This book misbehaves. Tokyo Kitchen Press, from where has this book come and where does it go? Please help me to leave it behind.

Fuck. You. Who the fuck do you think you are? You think you can just dither about for so many pages hinting at every other turn of some emotional catastrophe, of several emotional catastrophes, and leave all the details buried under innuendo and pushed through black boxes of your own secret design? Where's the motherfucking catharsis man?! What's the point?

After reading this book I can't shake the feeling that something terrible has happened. What the fuck does that even mean? Do I mean that I get the feeling that something terrible has happened in the world while I've been reading? That several terrible somethings have happened somewhere some time ago? That something terrible happened to me that I'm not quite recalling? That something terrible happened as a result of my reading? How the hell would that even work?

The point here is that the book is garbage, that you are garbage for publishing such garbage. And don't bother acting innocent, like you don't know what I'm talking about, like you're just plucky proprietors. Your own damn book already lays that one to rest. Nobody is not implicated. You put this piece of shit together.

Hell, I don't even know the main character's name, or hardly anybody's names for that matter! And now I find myself forgetting the names of my friends and family who exist decidedly outside this damned stack of leaves. Everything's getting confused. Where the fuck am I? What fucking century is it for god's sake! Half the time I don't even know anymore. Without considering the preposterous notion, I look back in the book for where the confusion started. What the fuck is that?

And that's not even the worst of it. I mean shit, it's bad enough that I'm still reading this shit trying to find my way out of it again. But then I get to that scene I keep hearing about. I know you know what I mean. The melt factory, or whatever the fuck it's called. All those dirty blank faces in one condemned building. And I'm supposed to get straight whose problems are whose? What's the fucking point? Except that one, right? You know. The one guy whose "clothes are still clean" and who "keeps on crying without remembering why"? Fuck you. You think you know me? This shit isn't funny.

It wasn't my fault. I didn't know how sick she was. You think I wouldn't have found a way to pay for better doctors? She was always working too hard. She said it was just a headache.

Look, I'm not trying to be an asshole here. But it's not right. I didn't agree to this. Just take me out of it. If you already know so much about me then you know I don't have the money to sue your ass and frankly that's not my style anyway. But you have got to get me out of it. I don't need this fucking reminder. Look, you don't even have to change every copy. I don't need a retraction or a reprint; just send me my own copy and leave me out of it. Please, just get me out of this book. She said it was just a headache.

DEAR TOKYO KITCHEN PRESS —

Let me be clear: I have loved my time with *Dismembrance*. I find no fault with the novel. Which is not to say that I consider it perfect. It is not a perfect novel. I am not even certain that it is a novel. You are familiar with the widespread debate regarding its status as such. I myself am well versed in such conversation, having made it my humble business to know what minds more agile than my own have to add, but while I have yet to determine for myself where I come down on the issue, I have forged happily ahead in uncertainty and imperfection. I have thoroughly enjoyed these past years of reading. Like so many others I have made a habit of spreading my reading of *Dismembrance* as far as the novel stretches. I have watched each film adaptation thus far professionally released as well as countless amateur films available online. I have seen performance pieces and gallery exhibits. I have participated in dinner theaters and found them worth the price of admission. I have slept many nights in and around the Watts Towers, sharing passages with passersby as well as the more permanent of fixtures. I have followed The Archive with a fervor approaching religious devotion. But just as the explorer's journey so often ends ultimately in a return to home, so have I come back time and again to the TKP edition, where I began. And while none of these credentials makes me unique amongst the readership of this very particular novel, likewise being in such good company does nothing to diminish my authority (quite the contrary in fact) on the subject of the text and its consequences. And there are consequences. And so, my own happy forging notwithstanding, I must say that although the fault may not lie with the novel, still there is fault to be found.

And here is where, despite my distaste for confrontation, I come to the point of this missive: Tokyo Kitchen Press, you must discontinue all printing and distribution of *Dismembrance*, post-haste. I realize this is no small request I make. Please understand I do not make it lightly. I understand that *Dismembrance* has been a strong seller for you, one that has raised the profile of your operation to the stature it enjoys today. It is not my intention to single you out amongst the many publishers, venues, individual artists, and amateur enthusiasts that contribute to the larger body of the novel; communiqués much like this one even now are on their way to several other points in the network of *Dismembrance*. Nor do I expect to issue commands and watch from a position of relative distance and safety, standing on high ground so to speak. The flood carries us all and I am implicated in the life of the novel, as are all of its readers. I will not shroud myself in the guise of spectating. I have taken great pains to do my part. Already to date I have purchased and destroyed some three thousand plus copies of various editions (the bulk of them yours, though you must understand this as nothing more than a manifestation of your relative prominence among the many outlets through which the public gains access to the text). I will continue this practice at the rate that my finances allow. I can say nothing definite regarding the recent spate of bomb threats that have disrupted several performances and exhibitions of work related to the novel though I have no doubt the purveyor of said threats must share with me some fundamental understanding of the dangers posed by *Dismembrance*. The same applies to the unfortunate events surrounding certain screenings at last year's Sundance Film Festival and the recent mishap at your own offices, the details of which I need not go into here. But unfortunate as such collateral damage may be, *Dismembrance* must be stopped. It can only end in fire.

Self-evident as the necessity of what I ask appears to me, I have come to understand that there are those who would call the novel harmless. Some believe the novel is nothing more than words on pages, despite the ways the novel has already seeped tangibly into the world around it. Having read the compendium released by Tokyo Kitchen Press in 2011 I know you are not so naïve. The only conclusion I can draw is that you believe the novel can be controlled despite its obvious inclinations toward expansion and permeation. While the novel's intentions and motivations may as yet be unclear, its activity is at the least ominous, at worst pestilential and pandemic. Though I am hopeful that you will see the truth in what I say, even now I hear the voice of the dissenting minority calling, 'Evidence! Evidence! Convince us!' I will not fail you.

In just the past 25 months there have been no fewer than 750 anonymous posts on The Archive from readers proclaiming themselves protagonist of *Dismembrance*, with each month's total increasing over the last. Besides the obvious falsity of such proclamations, this trend is disturbing for the possibility that it is not a result of the nationwide—I am still in pursuit of reliable global statistics and will of course pass them along just as soon as they are available—increase in cases of dementia but rather the driving force behind it. Or rather, simply another manifestation of the force that drives the widespread decay we see around us.

Every day I see independent vendors of questionable repute turning a good profit passing off glued stacks of metal slugs as traces viable for implantation who do not, despite my repeated attempts at calm persuasion, desist. I have managed in some cases to stop the odd perpetrator here or there (do not ask me how; such details are better left to oblivion, but rest assured that each success is a win for the reality that *Dismembrance* is even at this moment attempting to undermine), but the vast majority remains unfazed and undeterred.

Still today families toss lines off the Venice Pier though no one recalls the last caught fish. Informal survey (yet another aspect of the ongoing battle against *Dismembrance* that I have taken upon myself, on behalf of us all) reveals that while some do (erroneously) report reeling in a fish now and then, the only sea life to have been hauled over the railing in the last few years are sand sharks, which is of course a lie, if an inadvertent one, sand shark being a common term for the commonly appearing Rhinobatos rhinobatos—more simply known as the common guitar ray fish—which is both off-putting in appearance and devoid of edible meat save for four small strips near the tail.

And despite my best efforts to document my involvement with the novel, from my early salad days of blissful enjoyment to the era of my evolving understanding of the novel's finer impossibilities to my eventual recognition of its inherent dangers, I find my memory of life with *Dismembrance* growing if not dimmer then at the least less coherent with each passing day. If not for the volume in which I keep my reading notes—a painstakingly refined and revised facsimile of the first copy of the TKP edition with which I had contact, containing all possible chronological arrangements of the novel's action and enhanced with new passages reflecting the most important episodes of my life since the day I first broke the novel's spine—I might soon have no functioning record of these past years against which to monitor my recollections. And life before the novel, there was the boat. Teru. And others I didn't know, a harbor.

It's all in pieces, smells like salt water warmed in the interstices, fish and gasoline. But Teru sailed. It doesn't come together into context anymore, but the pings and clinks of metal clips and clasps holding jibs not quite becalmed and the bilge and a berth, a berth, and a catamaran. Catamaran? The words gloat on the surface, their meaning long since bleached by the sun. Catamaran catamaran, jib, bilge, berth. They sound. There was Teru. And rowing the dinghy in circles. Dogvane and catboat. Am I making this up? Dread not. The cut splice held too tight. Furled. And rowing in dingy circles growing smaller.

Tokyo Kitchen Press, you sea? My scrivening grows more difficult with each passing day. Did I say that already? Soon I fear the novel will have taken everything from me. Did I already? Life before *Dismembrance* comes in fits and flashes and starts and stops. Did you know, Tokyo Kitchen Press, that you can walk across the thinnest part of the surf, as far as it reaches up the shore, and feel the sand suck away beneath the soles of your feet as each wave recedes and ceases to be a thing separate from, with a name other than, the ocean? This evacuation pulls at me from the inside. I fear soon I will buckle around the emptiness, collapse, perhaps even bloom again when I am finished with my withering, reborn as a black hole, a lotus ripe for consumption, drawing all around me into my absence.

I am adrift. There is a message in this novel.

Tokyo Kitchen Press, there are still countless sextant copies of *Dismembrance* in circulation or in hiding. They must be found. The novel must be stopped. Readers across the country and, increasingly, around the world continue to extend the novel's reach. I will continue to do my part—as I've often said, I can handle anything in this life as long as it has nothing to do with either space or time—but you must do yours. Should the novel be allowed to continue into the hands and minds of readers at its current pace, I fear the damage soon will be irrevocable. Sincerely.

HARDENING ABSENCE[1]

NO, THAT WASN'T IT. Woke up at 3:45 yes.[2] It was yes Wednesday.
Yes windows covered. No light coming in to betray the time's meaning.
Though again it might've not bothered, the duct tape, the drapes. The lights
buzzed outside the windows all night. The difference was only in quality of.
But that wasn't when the remembering began; it was when the forget

---

[1] Recognized by many readers as the closest text we have to the midpoint of the character's
trajectory over the course of the chronological narrative, the excerpt included here marks
the start (save for a copy of a receipt for one prodigious order of Chinese food—Kung Pao
Chicken, Duck Fantasy, Green Beans in Garlic Sauce, Chinese Broccoli in Oyster Sauce,
Shrimp Fried Rice, Stir Fried Egg and Tomato, Hot and Sour Soup, Pork Bao, Chicken Chow
Mein, Salt and Pepper Shrimp—not included here) of the novel's second volume in the TKP
edition. At the same time, some independent compilers both online and operating small
presses position the excerpt as the start of the entire collected text.

[2] You woke up stiff at 3:47. It was a Wednesday; you know that now. 3:47, meant a.m. or p.m.?
The windows were dark, curtains pulled tight, held down with duct tape. You didn't know what
Wednesday was, what 3:47 meant, what when meant. Now you've recalled it, from where? But
then you didn't know. Your mouth knew the sticky dry smack of thirst. Your nose smelled seared
something. You remember now that then you'd gone on eating even after you didn't know to eat,
know why to eat, know how. You didn't know. Maybe you choked. Did you forget to swallow?
Forget how? Did that start you back the other way? But you did eat, shat only in one corner of

How long did that bowl of cereal sit, waiting for spoon that hung suspended in? Long enough that the mush it held had long since ceased to be anything other than the mush it had become by the time it drew attention. Of what had thoughts been thinking all that time the mush was becoming? Nothing. Not that there were none, was no, thoughts, thinking. But thoughts of nothing, a particular nothing, a nothing with heft and weight and a shape not quite sharp enough to name, an outline that only announced absence.

They were gone. How? To where? No traumatic event to point to, no moment of rupture or act of separation. There was simply a time when they were and then a time when they weren't. The traces they'd left behind proved them. Artifacts of presence. Swirls of hair dried to shower wall, deformed spiders crisp on white tile, troubling the straight lines of worn grout. The fading scent on pillows, blankets, coats hanging in closets, of bodies. Dishes leaning in the sink that might've been theirs. A stuffed grey toy, kicked out of foot's path, left beneath a couch or, then replaced, to be kicked again.

The investigation was a late bloomer and non-starter. First, not enough time gone by. Though they were clearly gone, even despite the ways they were not. Absence gains resonance over time, but presence is still a toggle switch. Then, no indication of foul play. No bodies to make murder. No evidence of abduction. Absence, it turns out, is no crime, not punishable. And anyway, what were their names?

Absence gains resonance, grows solid, saturated, hard like a tumor, calcified by the catalogue of memories surrounding it, standing out inside the tight lines of a topographical map. Sunday, awake at 3:35, sun not up, piss one, brush teeth, bowl of cereal, piss two and shit slow, phone calls (not quite like

---

the room. Sat on the floor, didn't know chairs. How do you know 3:47 if the numbers weren't numbers then? But you remember it all, all the coming back. You've accumulated it all since in a blurry origin point somewhere just before.

But now you're certain there's more, before the origin, behind the back wall of what you can remember. There must be more; you weren't always what you are. You know it. You know from disinterested context that surrounds you and what you've accumulated. You must've been someone once, must've been a. The television was on, has always been. You got a lot that way. Got far enough to

conversation) with police at 5:45, 6:32, 7:50, each one shorter than the last, hard to explain, drinking by 9, no help, piss three, with water running stare at the toothbrush bent in the bristles and faded, the one that feels wrong in your mouth, nothing to do so lunch early at eleven, oatmeal tasteless, no matter, go on. Monday, up at 4:15. Tuesday, 3:20. Wednesday 5 exactly. Thursday. Friday. Saturday. Rinse and repeat. Stare at the toothbrush. That side of the bed, empty. The pillow lost its smell on the thirty-third day.

Fall arrived. In the mail came a check refunding tuition[3]—one student few, and two credit card offers, preapproved, and a magazine—of advertisements masquerading as stories of human interest and profiles of places, tips for a traveling lifestyle—from an auto insurance company, and a quarterly statement on a retirement portfolio. It means.

Absence grows hard around the edges. Tumors become inoperable. The only option ended up scorched earth. First it was pawning them away. Them and them. The memories left and the edges of the absence fuzzed. Chinese takeout was how it started. An overly ambitious order and a delivery boy with itchy red eyes. The money wasn't there anymore. Where was even a wallet at that point? No way to pay.

Cash or credit, no exceptions, he said.

You can't have the food if you can't pay, he said.

---

[3] Spanish Mandarin Academy, Mid-Wilshire Christian Academy, Page Private School, Wonderland School, Media Center Montessori Preschool, St. Francis Xavier School, Stepping Stones Montessori School, Study Circle Preschool and Kindergarten, Viewpoint School, Great Beginning, Our Lady of The Assumption School, Saint Albert The Great School, Turning Point School, Li'l Toots Preschool, New Life Christian Academy, Saint Lucy School, Diamond Bar Montessori Academy, Happy Land School, Immaculate Conception School, Immaculate Heart School, Immaculate Heart of Mary School, Kabbalah Children's Academy, Giant Step Learning Center, Marcus Garvey School, Nativity School, New Langston Hughes Academy, Resurrection School, The Tikva Tots, Der Kinder Garden, Shield of Faith Christian School and New Roads School have all at one time or another been posited as the real world inspiration for the school first mentioned here and appearing again later in the novel, though to date no definitive answer has been accepted.

He said, Well if you have to have it then,

It looked like a roll of quarters. A tiny Tower of Pisa. Tired from leaning.

We'll call it even, he said.

It's not like how they talk about it on the news. Not at first anyway. A pinch in the brainpan, a something you thought you saw out of the corner of your eye. Hard even to know that anything's gone. Those who are not present cannot raise their hands. It'd be easier to see later, further down the rabbit hole, except by then there's no looking. And no receipt.

THE ANNOTATED AMYGDALOIDS

BY

PAUL CHOWDER

WHEN ASKED BY the editors of the *Compendium*'s second edition
for permission to include transcriptions of lyrics from their latest album,
The River Lethe, The Amygdaloids had this[1] to say about the influence of
Dismembrance on their work: "Our music is about brain, mind, and mental
disorder. *Dismembrance* goes far in exploring the humanistic implications
of scientific advancement and the inextricability of brain, mind, body, and
person. As scientist musicians, this approach speaks to us and so we choose
to speak back to the novel with this album. Past lovers often leave strong
and enduring memories. Novels do the same. Sometimes we have memories
that we can't get rid of. In post-traumatic stress disorder, these can be
debilitating. Songs like "A Trace" tell stories about this. We've done research
in rats showing that a specific memory can be deleted by carefully timing
the retrieval of that memory with a drug, a so-called "Memory Pill." Echoes
of this and other experiments on the leading edge of scientific research into
memory abound in the novel, hence the name of that song. Many readers
will recognize the scientific themes of fuzzy trace theory and new ideas on
reconsolidation underlying much of the novel. We felt that the Amygdaloids,

---

[1] As The Amygdaloids were not in fact available for comment at time of press, the included
quotation has been fabricated by the editors for the purposes of the *Compendium*.

as fans of the novel, were well positioned to engage with the novel and add to the growing interdisciplinarity of the response to the novel coming from a number of communities, literary, scientific, artistic, pop, alt, subverse, and so on. Dismembrance is a novel that implicates the reader in its own existence. You can't walk away from it once you begin to wonder whether it might not in fact be about you. And so, simply put, The River Lethe is our attempt to assist in the rewriting of what's been forgotten.
—J. LeDoux

"...looks interesting. I'm not sure I follow what is going where. Is the thing by Paul Chowder supposed to be fictional? I assume so since I don't remember giving these quotes. If so, could you put a note somewhere in your foreword or preface that the comments by The Amygs were part of the fictional narrative and were not real comments. I will read through the notes when I have some time."
—J. LeDoux

Hello, it's me again.
—P. Chowder

Piece of My Mind
—J. LeDoux

I was gonna give you a piece of my mind[2]

---

[2] I'm sorry. I have to apologize for that up there. I was going to say more by way of introduction, but then I thought I might as well get right to it. After all, do you really need me to explain that I'm going to annotate these lyrics by this band? I mean, you already saw the title, "THE ANNOTATED AMYGDALOIDS" and you saw the "by Paul Chowder," which really is a bit of a misnomer come to think of it. Yes it's true, I am going to write these annotations, and likely it can be presumed that these annotations I will write to these lyrics will offer some insight into said lyrics and that the novel that is the occasion of this whole *Compendium* (and thank God, by the way, that I am not the one who has to edit this puff pastry of a whole as it crumbles in the hands), but really is it fair to say that the whole shebang is "by" me? Look again and you'll see that each song was in fact written by one "J. LeDoux," himself a verifiable Amygdaloid. Granted I'm still on the first line of the first song of 12 total on the album, and granted by the look of this first footnote you wouldn't be outside the realm of plausibility to suggest that I will end up by the

But I wouldn't have enough for me[3]

You wore out my brain so it's hard to find[4]

---

end (assuming I do in fact get to the end) having written substantially more words in total than did J. LeDoux himself, but whatever number you predict I'll write, there will still be a fraction of the words in "THE ANNOTATED AMYGDALOIDS" that are not by me.

[3] Suppose for instance that I end up writing 5,000 words of annotations. That sounds like enough. Not that I'm planning to write 5,000 words, but just suppose I do. I was going to say 5,347 words but that is such a specific number it might seem to you I'm up to something, like say perhaps I've already written those 5,347 words and am now going back to write this early entry to give myself the air of extremely accurate offhanded numerical estimation. A knack for which I readily admit I do not have. And then, if I had done that, wouldn't these words throw off that 5,347 so that in fact now it's something more like 5,449? And it would only keep getting thrown further off as I continued, so that eventually I would be forced to go back and change that original 5,347 to 5,582, which means I would have to change that 5,449 to 5,684, and so on. But you see the problem. It'd only keep going. It'd never end, the need to go back and change what I'd done to fit what I did later, which I'd also have to change, which would make it necessary to go back again. So clearly 5,347 was just an arbitrary number I came up with right in that moment (the first time I typed it) to illustrate a point. What point exactly? Wait a moment; I'll find it. Ah yes (I had to read back), I remember now. The point was that 5,347 might come across as a real number arrived at by actual counting. Though I suppose that wasn't the point I ended up making at all. Still, 5,000. It has the feel of a stand-in doesn't it? An estimation rather than a calculation. Which is ridiculous because after all 5,000 is no more or less specific a number than 5,347. Or 5,449 or any of the others for that matter. Each of them is just one number. But 5,000, with all those zeroes, it looks more like a placeholder than a number. It should be in quotes, "5,000." When you read it imagine my fingers, index and middle of each hand, tapping an invisible bar of air floating horizontally six inches out in front of my face. "5,000." You see, it's not really 5,000; we'll just call it that.

[4] So if I wrote "5,000" words, and say the lyrics of the songs consisted of 350 words—excuse me, I mean "350" words—then I would only have written 93.5 percent of the total words. And even though that figure is meaningless in the sense that I didn't (won't) write 5,000 words and the lyrics are not a total of 350 words so 93.5 percent (which is the percent of the total words I would claim responsibility for in that imaginary scenario) is really a fictional (though accurate—I used a calculator and rounded up) percentage, it does still manage to mean something doesn't it? Whatever the real numbers might be the picture is instructive. It's one of those graphs where the line swoops up and looks like it'll intersect with one of the axes just off frame if you could only follow it that far. Except it never does. There's a limit that can't be reached. No matter how many words I write, I'll never be able to claim authority over them all. It's called an asymptote.

A piece of my mind that's free[5]
You left so little of my mind behind[6]
I can hardly remember me[7]
I mostly have to pantomime[8]
The one I used to be

---

[5] Free indeed. I can't believe I'm not being paid for this. I could use the money. Not that writing annotations for some song lyrics about a book for a second book collecting writings about the first book would bring with it some really impressive amount of cash, but just a little something would've been nice. Just a few hundred or so, just enough to maintain the "paid writer" thing. But of course there's not much money to be made in literary criticism, hardly more than in poetry come to think of it, so I don't know where I'd expect them to get the money. And who's ever heard of Tokyo Kitchen Press? I certainly haven't. Not that I know every small press there is, or even most of them, but I have been wandering around in this literary business for some time, longer perhaps than I care to remember, and one would think it likely I'd have come across it at one time or another before now. All of which is to say that no I don't suppose I ought to have been offered any money for this. Come to think of it, how did those unenvied editors ever think of asking me to write these annotations at all? Is it possible they haven't heard what a fraud I am? That I can't write a thing to save my life? Blood from a turnip and all that? Or was it water from a stone? Or is it stone soup? Whatever the case, how could they possibly have faith that I'd come through? Which reminds me, perhaps I'd better move on.

[6] And here is where we get to the main problem, if you'll allow me to turn your attention to the novel for a moment. Though I suppose I'd understand if you feel somewhat caught off guard by such a turn; nothing in the title "THE ANNOTATED AMYGDALOIDS" really quite suggests that we'd be getting into talking about a book. You might even be feeling misled, perhaps even mildly betrayed, particularly with my credibility on rather precarious ground after that whole "by Paul Chowder" fiasco. Though at the same time I suppose it'd be fair to point out that all of it, the Amygdaloids and the Annotations—however you want to allocate authorship—exists within the larger context of the *Compendium*, which is pretty clear about where its gaze lies wouldn't you say? And though I'm only now making this move to really focus on the novel, I imagine that other pieces in the *Compendium* once it's been collected will be more punctual about getting to the point than am I.

[7] There, you see? This makes it more clear, doesn't it? Good old J. LeDoux really came through with that line, didn't he? Now you see why "THE ANNOTATED AMYGDALOIDS" actually belongs in this *Compendium*. Or at least you see why the Amygdaloids belong. You're probably less certain about the annotations, and really I can't blame you.

[8] This is probably as good a point as any at which to make a confession. Or no, actually scratch that. Let's try a hypothetical instead. Let's say I never read the book. I know, crazy right? But let's just say. Suppose I didn't. How might you react? Would you stop reading immediately upon learning of my implied deception? I say implied because after all I never did say I read it.

28

My brain's a tangled mess[9]
Ever since you got in it
You took the very best[10]
Just as you intended

No one ever asked. Everyone just assumed. Just like you did, right? And you know what they say about making assumptions. But then, the premise of this entry into the *Compendium* does sort of rest on that assumption, or at least imply and allude to it, so maybe it's safe to say that I'm more to blame for this than you are. I mean, I would be more to blame, hypothetically speaking.

[9] But you're still reading I see. Or I don't see. I don't have eyes. I'm just these words on these pages now (now?). So I don't see that you're reading still, but if you are then I'm right, and if you aren't then you don't know I'm wrong. And you won't know I'm wrong until you go on reading, at which point I'll be right. Funny how that works, isn't it? But really, thank you for reading. Did I say that already?

[10] When Roz left she only took one book with her. I wanted to take it as a sign that she wouldn't be away long and suggested as much. She said she only needed the one as seed to put on a shelf in her new place. I didn't like the idea of her putting down roots someplace else, but I had no illusions that it was up to me. I remembered all of that while I was looking just now at the bookshelf I've set up to the left of my desk up here in the barn. It's too small really, just one of those fold-up jobs that's all one articulated apparatus—a back, sides that swing out, and shelves that flip down. It's really just some sticks of wood, three short planks, and a sufficient number of metal hinges, but the ratio of utility to volume of material is hard to beat. Part of that may have to do with the fact that a bookshelf's primary function is to organize a bit of empty space, but I appreciate the design nonetheless. But what I really like about this shelf beyond its utility, simplicity, and portability (so easy to carry when it's folded up), is the fact that the more you use it the more solid it becomes. As soon as you fold out the sides and flip down the shelves it all locks into shape. To break it down you first have to flip the shelves back up and then you can fold the sides back in against the back, so the more books you've got on it, the less possible it is for the shelf to disaggregate back into its components. The same cannot be said for shelves put up on a wall with brackets. The more books you put onto those sorts of shelves, the closer they come to collapse. But this little number I've got here, the more I ask of it, the more steadfast it grows. I can almost see it digging its heels into the floor and setting its jaw. It's only about four feet tall so it's not likely to fall forward (it came with little metal bits designed to anchor it to the wall, but that struck me as more work than my relative lack of concern calls for) unless we have an earthquake, which I don't expect because really earthquakes are essentially unfathomable at any moment other than the moment in which they are occurring. Each of the three shelves is a row of bad teeth in a crowded mouth, packed tight, all different heights and widths. Resting on top of each jagged row is what I consider a reasonable scattering of books slid sideways into the space

Why are you like that[11]
I wish that I knew
What goes on inside your brain
Makes you make me blue[12]
You say you want to change[13]

---

between the teeth and the underside of the shelf above. Of course the top shelf has no shelf above it, it's the top shelf, meaning I could stack the sideways books as high as physics and my unsteady hands allow, but I've opted to restrain myself and leave the top shelf with a thin layer that matches the lower shelves—otherwise it'd look out of balance. There's also a small strip of space between the bottom shelf and the floor on which the whole contraption stands and I've filled that as well, a bit tighter even since the floor is flat and allows for more dense stacking and packing. With the mouth and tooth imagery, I feel compelled to point out that they're all bottom teeth. Books sit on shelves, not the other way around (though full as my shelves are, one could certainly be forgiven for thinking so at first glance), so I needn't worry about any of the sideways books getting chewed. All around the shelf's uniform front-facing plane I've got smallish to tallish piles of books in twisted stacks plus a few more here and there leaning at jaunty angles either against the bookshelf itself or against one of the crowd of surrounding stacks, all doing their best to look nonchalant. Counting the rows of teeth, plus what's been slid in sideways, plus those stacked or standing nearby, I've got this shelf running at about 147 percent capacity. And yes that's only an estimate; I didn't really count all the teeth. It's not important how overclocked the shelf is. It's much more worthy of notice that overstuffed and surrounded, the bookshelf actually looks like it's being guarded by the books, as if they're huddling protectively close, a herd of elephants all mother and sister backing themselves into a thick circle around their babies. Though given the enduring gender imbalance in literature I suppose I might as well toss that metaphor too.

While I was remembering I realized that I don't know which book she took, or if I did know that I don't remember anymore. I went back to the house and stood in front of the shelves in the living room. I thought maybe I'd be able to see the hole where the book had been and somehow recognize what'd filled that space, that a translucent image transposed in my memory over that blank might reveal enough for me to know, but of course I couldn't, it didn't, I don't. Each empty space was unique in its shape, defined by adjacent books leaning in from the sides or ones that sat stacked above or below. But while a careful examination of the outline of absence drawn by presence made clear that something was missing, it gave me no clue about what that something was.

[11] I wish I knew.

[12] I'm feeling a bit down today. What a funny thing to write. Not the part about feeling down; that's not really funny at all, more melancholy than anything. Cheap ennui. But today, what does that mean? I know what it meant when I typed it; I know what day it is.

You want to settle down
That I'm the one you want[14]
To be with in a gown
There you go again,[15]
Putting me down to your friends
Don't you realize[16]

But what can it possibly mean to you, whoever you are? You don't really know what referent it had when I typed it and I don't really know what referent it had when you read it just now. Just now? Just then? What differánce does it make? It's nearly enough to make you stop trying. It's Tuesday by the way.

[13] Doesn't everyone? Even the people with the most money and the straightest teeth and the most well-behaved children and the best-decorated homes probably only got all that money and those teeth and those robotic children and uncomfortable homes because they were trying to change themselves from the poor ugly slobs they thought they were. And now I've revealed more about myself than I probably meant to. Funny how I said probably meant to instead of probably revealed, as if the thing in question was not how much you can guess about me but rather my intentions.

[14] Of course the things we change about ourselves rarely turn out to be the things we really wanted to change. It's amazing any of us make it through middle school at all.

[15] Yes, I've gotten so far off course. I was going to say that I've gotten off course again, but that would make it sound like I was on course at some point, then got off, then somehow got back on again, and then got off again. But really I started off on the wrong foot as usual, talking about myself when I was supposed to be saying something about this song and the connections it draws to/from the novel. So no, I'm not off course again; I'm only off course still. The editors probably won't even want to use any of this. They'll have to ask someone else to write these annotations. Or not these annotations since these annotations are such crap, but other annotations, annotations that actually do the job they were meant to do.

[16] I read this line just now, after having been distracted yet again. Usually when I do that I back up a few lines to get a sort of running start, to get back the thread you know? Only this time I didn't do that; I just read the line after the last line I'd read without reading that last line again, or any of the lines before it. Don't you realize. And in order to tell you about it as I've just done, I had to put a period at the end of that line, though there wasn't one really. And now that I've taken the time to read the line again along with the one before it and the one after it (I know you can't tell from reading this that I did actually take that time, but trust me, I did) I realize that I didn't even need that running start anyway. The previous line seems to want a period at its end so really the line in question can start on its own just fine. The real issue is the jump from this line (Don't you realize) to the next. If I read the two lines together I get the feeling that there's a question mark hiding there at the end of that next line. And

Words are means not[17] ends
No matter what you say
You will still be you
If you wanna change who you are
You gotta change what you do
I was gonna give you a piece of my mind
But I wouldn't have enough for me
You wore out my brain so it's hard to find
A piece of my mind that's free
You left so little of my mind behind[18]

---

if I hadn't gotten distracted thinking about the running start I didn't get I would've realized that, but instead I stopped at the end of the line and so I read it as if it had the period I gave it. Don't you realize. And thanks to that period that wasn't there, I read it not as the first part of a question but as an imperative, an instruction. Don't you realize. The line sort of puts one hand on its hip and wags a finger in my face a bit, like a parent warning a child not to misbehave. Don't you realize (or else). So I guess I better not.

[17] Is it just me or is this really more of an "and also" sort of moment?

[18] And here is where we get to the main problem. Did I say that already? With the novel I mean. Sorry, somehow I keep wanting to assume that you know what I'm talking about, as if you're not a reader coming to this from your own life and time, which has nothing (necessarily) to do with my life and time, since these annotations are really sort of cut loose from time aren't they? I mean, once I've written them (as much as anyone ever writes anything) and before you've written them yourself (as much as reading writes everything), I think they all sort of float separately from the passage of time, lumps of clay about to hit the spinning wheel. No way to know which way they'll fly, or if they'll stick. Which means that although I'm writing this now as time passes, once I stop it becomes a sort of time capsule in suspended animation (a clumsy metaphor I know, but it appeals to a younger version of myself that once saved box tops for decoder rings and drew treasure maps with lemon juice) and doesn't really reenter human time—human time, that's an odd phrase. A rather human-centric thing to say I guess. Maybe better to say linear time. Suggests a helpful guideline and makes no claim to ownership. Yes, I say it doesn't reenter linear time again until you're reading it. And even then it gets tangled up in time while you read it, but at the very same time the clay is still out there floating, waiting for somebody else to read it, which could happen at any moment and which would get it all fumbled up into some other time.

I can hardly remember me[19]

I mostly have to pantomime[20]

---

[19] I imagine you're probably familiar with the social scenario in which you acknowledge a person waving and calling to you, only to belatedly realize you were not the intended recipient of the acknowledged communiqué. You've either seen the gag in film and TV or worse, it's happened to you. It happened to me. I had turned twelve that summer. The junior high school shared a bus stop with the high school. A friend of my sister, my older sister, an older than me friend of my three years older sister, waved to me from a car. From the window of a slowly passing car, a friend of my sister waved to me as I stood at the bus stop after school. I know this is what happened, though really I couldn't swear to most of those details. I know my sister is three years older than I am. At least, I have it from trusted sources. And all of her friends were older than me too of course. But was I twelve? Maybe I was in high school. Was it after school, at the bus stop? It was probably at the bus stop. But maybe I wasn't standing; maybe I was walking. Maybe the person who really got that wave hello was moving too. Maybe that movement behind my back, that movement of whose existence I knew nada, was the key to the gag that duped me; three objects in motion creating the illusion of a center. Whatever the case, I know what happened, though I remember none of those details. What I do remember is the sudden contortion in her face as her eyes shifted their depth of focus from intended seeing to inadvertent noticing. A smile snapped down into revolted confusion, which was probably more confusion and less revulsion, but I was twelve so I wouldn't have seen that. I remember the whipshock of embarrassment as I switched from perceiving my reality to perceiving her reality. It's not the shock of jumping into a cold pool. Nor is it the shock of being pushed. It's the shock of the pool jumping at you from behind, or realizing you were in the pool the whole time. It's stepping up onto a last step that isn't there, or down onto one you weren't expecting. Except that stairs can't look back at you with disbelieving horror at the mere thought that your friend's little brother might have thought you were trying to say hello to him. Am I projecting? Maybe the real point here is that all these details I think I really do really remember are even less reliable than the ones I don't remember but know to be true. A look on someone's face in a passing car? A momentary flash of adolescent embarrassment? How could I possibly hope to accurately render these things in words through so many decades of living with the memory? Who knows what her face looked like? It could've been mildly quizzical. Perhaps nonplussed. Am I really sure this happened to me? Or have I simply watched too many iterations of the gag in media and maybe managed to write the plot into a piece of a dream I thought I once had? I've clearly left certainty behind long since. The remembering is much longer than the moments in which things happen. And I heard that girl died some time ago.

[20] Roz thinks that that thing I do, where I act like we're old friends even though all you are to me is the fear of my failure as a writer and all I am to you is a bunch of words on a page,

The one I used to be[21]
The one I used to be[22]

---

she says I do it all the time, not just when I'm writing. I suppose it's the narrative equivalent of expecting someone to help with the dishes the first time they've come to your house for dinner. Not totally out of the realm of possibility, but not to be expected exactly. Come to think of it, I wouldn't really expect anybody to help with the dishes in that scenario, but if I imagine myself as the reader instead I can certainly think of some books I've read that make me want to help with the dishes. And now this metaphor's gone on so long it's beginning to lose coherency isn't it? Or maybe it's only me losing resolution. You see, after that sentence about imagining myself as the reader, I stopped to think of authors I'd like to help in the kitchen. I had a short list going. The names come easily; the hard part was deciding what we ate, and what sort of dishes we used, and whether I'd clear the table or stand at the sink. Whether I'd wash or rinse or dry. I probably wouldn't put away, unless I were in the home of a book who was fine with me putting things wherever I may. And there you probably noticed that I switched from thinking of authors to thinking of books. Which is ridiculous if you try to imagine helping a book in the kitchen with the dishes after dinner and is even more ridiculous if you try to imagine reading a book having anything to do with the person who wrote it. There's more obviously, but none of this is the point. The point of course is that I stopped to think. And if I'm being totally honest I have to admit that I made a sandwich while I was thinking. All the dinner and kitchen stuff, it got me hungry. And while I stopped, what did this text do? It didn't do anything. For all I know it ceased to exist. So you see, even as I'm writing it a text really has not much at all to do with time.

[21] Last night I dreamed I stood on the hump of a low grassy hill. And on the last step down into a basement filled with bassinets. And in the doorway of a shop filled with empty shelves. And with my back against a wall, not knowing my own home. And in a deep well counting the stars in the small circle above me called sky. And on a wide field of tangled arms and legs reaching out in every direction as far as bodies can break.

[22] Flames painted the dark, exhausted themselves in whorls of smoke. The ashes of dead memories landed on the lashes of my stinging eyes. Tears came unbidden at the sight of all the rows of infants not even pushing against the walls of their too small crates, never speaking, never spoken to, the beginnings of their individualized selves pumped from them, not learning like a baby is supposed to do but generating the preverbal memories that are the luxury of the deep pocketed, forced to forget themselves in the midst of their becoming. I wanted not to wonder what they did with these almost children once they no longer fit the cramped confines of this grotesque farm. Amongst the empty shelves of the pawnshop I scanned for the things I couldn't recall. And found none. On unfamiliar walls I looked for familiar places inside framed photographs, found the face from the medicine cabinet's mirror

The one I used to be[23]
The one I used to be[24]
The one I used to be[25]

[Though the complete text of Mr. Chowder's annotations was not ready at time of press, the editors thank him for his contribution to this second edition and look forward with relish to its completion, whether it be in time for the third edition or any after. —T.K.P.]

---

mugging for the camera. I prowled, opened drawers with the voyeur's guilty thrill, tried on the clothes I found in the closet, tried on the names I read on pieces of paper, looked over my shoulder for no one to come back and call me intruder. Trying to remember is counting from the bottom of a well the blades in a nearby field of grass. Shaking the hands and kicking the feet of dismembered pieces of people I might have been, I found myself afraid to remember, not knowing what I'd lost.

[23] Last night I dreamed I was an octopus. I injected my prey with paralysis and confusion to stop its struggling. I watched my arms enfold, felt the tension of their embrace, hoped what they had in mind. In my many cups I tasted the fear of its letting go, preached patience to myself while I worked my beak, dismembering. Swallowing was slow, but in time I was made whole.

[24] Last night I dreamed I was consumed.

[25] Last night I dreamed someone read a book about me, not realizing it was me who was reading, while it was someone else's dream.

THE MAHABHARATA

[THE FOLLOWING EXCERPT, excluded from the TKP edition of 2007 as well as the first edition of the *Compendium* has, in the estimation of the editors, earned a place in this second edition thanks to its developing status as one of the most claimed and (re)created pieces of dismemorabilia vying for attention. It is the belief of the editors that The Mahabharata, as it has come to be known, is—regardless of (and for many readers precisely because of) the incertitude of its provenance and the resulting variety of its versions—not only worthy of inclusion here, but also in point of fact unquestionably a part of the novel. Though general consensus ascribes the earliest recorded mention of The Mahabharata to an obscure entry in The Archive from the winter of 2001,[1] the excerpt itself only began to garner more widespread attention after its appearance in an appendix to J.R. Sparrow's 2005 case study published by

---

[1] Submitted December 7th by commenter "kangi10," the enigmatic entry in its entirety reads, "Now I am become Ganesha, curator of worlds. The Mahabharata does not rest." As this was the first and last contribution to The Archive made by kangi10, the identity and motivation of the commenter are left to rumor and speculation. Similarly, though the significance of the comment continues to accrue as the conversation surrounding The Mahabharata and the novel as a whole grows, the original meaning intended by this self-proclaimed curator has been lost beneath the layering of time and the proliferation of varying readings.

Kannon Books, *Sacred and also Profane: Reading Dismembrance*. Subsequent appearances of The Mahabharata have grown quickly and steadily more frequent and heterogeneous. Some notable examples include an edition of the novel released in 2012 by Sahasranama Press in which The Mahabharata is presented as an invocation at the start of the text; The Mahabharata, a daily blog of haiku started in 2009 by independent recording artist Fat Man Cypher; The Mahabharata, an exhibit at the Museum of Jurassic Technology in Culver City, California consisting of a series of disparate versions of the text each printed on pressed grains of rice displayed on slides and viewed under microscopes; The Mahabharata, an ongoing three-panel comic strip appearing in The Archive weekly since September 2010, courtesy of username "Smritinoveda1000?!"; The Mahabharata, a stage play from Los Angeles-based arboreal acting troupe Shinrin Yoku which enjoyed modest success at small venues across the L.A. metro area from March-September 2006 and later enjoyed consecutive three-month runs in New York, Chicago, Seattle, and again Los Angeles in 2011; and The Mahabharata, first displayed in the debut exhibition of paper artist Parvati Williams in the spring of 2010 and later used as the cover image for Trident Books' edition of the novel released in early 2014. But while the volume of the conversation drawn by The Mahabharata's point of gravity is good reason for its inclusion in this new edition, the nature of conversation renders that inclusion problematic. Due to the wide variety of The Mahabharata's versions and the relative youth of the conversation surrounding them, a consensus on how best to represent the excerpt here has itself been a subject desiring some reflection. Given the limitations of time and of space and of spacetime, the editors have opted to present a composite text representing an approximate synthesis of available versions and/or records of versions no longer accessible. As this new version cannot fairly be attributed to any particular earlier purveyor of The Mahabharata, the excerpt here included—appropriately titled The Mahabharata—is provided courtesy of Tokyo Kitchen Press. –T.K.P.]

8:15. I'm a little boy. It was the summer of '45. Mom was four. Dad was still two years away. I started falling but never made it all the way down. The heat was tremendous.

They made a statue for me. Well, not for me, but you know, after me. I still remember the first time I saw it, but it's a memory that disappears each time

I notice it in the corner of my vision, leaving me sniffing a series of oblique details like fresh tracks. The girl I was with, the ridiculous sweater I was wearing, the feeling of being in my twenties. But the statue stuck with me somehow. A darkly burnished mother doubled over, clutching one child to her chest, scooping another up onto her back. I believed I saw in the statue something I hadn't understood before. Perhaps it was only a moment in which I remembered that I loved my mother, but either way, quite a statue. I recently saw that statue again for the first time. I was dismayed. It looked nothing like I felt then.

And then there's the cenotaph, which most people probably only see for what's written on it or what stands above it. Isn't that always the way? Trite, but what can you do? Still, I think it's the most appropriate. I mean does any of the rest of it really suffice? Sure there's the visceral reaction to all those jarred up keloids and broken watches and faded photos, shadows that don't work right and people signing their names at the end as if they've read anything at all. But the cenotaph with its emptiness is the only thing that's got space enough to hold it all, everything that can't be said, can't be incorporated into a sense of self. Otherwise there's just me, a tiny big red balloon hanging suspended over a model of an earlier version of the city that doesn't exist anymore and, let's face it, probably never did. Which of course we know can work on the page, but when I'm hanging there for all to see looking so much like a Tootsie Pop without my stick, well, it's hard for some people to fit their minds into something that tiny.

44.4 seconds I've been falling now. You'd think I was joking, such an unlucky number. And I still haven't made it all the way down. But it's too late to tell you any of this anyway; you won't hear, already, a massive dilation of time like brightest white

THE ARCHIVE UP IN FLAMES[1]

A BURNING, UP into the sky. And now there will be nothing. A spectacle, a blackout. An invisible grotesquery. The Archivist, me. It's all now. This, the end.

The burning looked like burning. The flames danced red, yellow, orange, blue or green, white at its most intense.[2] But what burned was only containers. Inside containers. Memories don't. There are no ashes to consume, to sit dryly in my mouth. They are nothing. And I am[3] obsolete. Will only spin fictions, or if I don't, won't know.

"You can be rebuilt," he said.

---

[1] The excerpt included here is commonly regarded as the "beginning" of the novel, if there is one, and is what appears on the first page of text in the TKP edition. The text has been adjusted for tense, pronoun usage, and readability.

[2] For an illuminating discussion of the rainbow's missing purple, the editors recommend the oft-cited essay Discolorance: Remembering What's Missing in Dismembrance (first published by What Books Press and later included in The Compendium's first edition) by Lucy M. Gale, founder and director of the California Syntext Initiative, and one of the leading contemporary voices on color theory and Dismembrance.

[3] is

He said, "You can be rebuilt."
I asked,
And he said, "It can be rebuilt."
And, "Yes, I can," I said. It wasn't true.
The heat was tremendous.

[This page left intentionally blank.]

FIG. 1
This page left intentionally blank.

FIG. 2
An Egg with No Shell

FIG. 3
Love[1], 1984
Michael Puig (1973-2000)
Acrylic on canvas

---

[1] Painting by Gorilla Michael. Photo by Ron Cohn, The Gorilla Foundation / koko.org

FIG. 4
Michael, 1997
Graphite on paper
Image courtesy of Tokyo Kitchen Press

FIG. 5
Figures 5

FIG. 6
The Light of The Sun

FIG. 7
A Vessel

FIG. 8
A Tootsie Pop without a stick.

FIG. 9
Water and Stone

FIG. 10
Water and Light

FIG. 11
Jars, empty.

FIG. 12

My mind wanders around into silly

APOCRYPHA

A MESSAGE FROM CASTOR P. ROSENTHAL

More than any of my earlier work, the pieces collected in *Watches from Nagasaki* enjoy a sort of enduring celebrity. Note that I do not claim that celebrity for myself. I realize the public's fascination is not with me but with the collection. It's all rather more zeitgeisty than I'd prefer, but the questions I am asked about *Watches* give the feeling of being an old childhood friend to someone now very famous; who I am is not so important as what answers I might possess.

What I describe may smell like any author's predicament, pungent with voyeurism. Rare is the author who hasn't been asked for the "answers" to what she has written, as if such answers could be anything other than what she has written. Even those who consistently reject the intentional fallacy, when given the opportunity, often find themselves asking what an author "meant" by this bit or that.

But these are not the questions that *Watches from Nagasaki* engenders because mine is not the text that anyone who reads it wants to solve. You might even say that *Watches from Nagasaki* has no readers; or that it is no text at all, or at least nothing separate from the novel it purports to explore. And although I am skeptical of its ability to make the novel any more (at all) transparent (opaque?) I accept its uniquely auxiliary existence. *Watches from Nagasaki* is, after all, for me (and I freely acknowledge the relative unimportance of my opinion on this matter), not a text I've written so much as a text I've read, which is to say it is my reading of *Dismembrance*.

And so I have no authorial answers to dole out. I am, in this case, no more than one among many readers of a novel that goes on generating questions while offering no answers. *Watches from Nagasaki* is my attempt to explore the questions the novel asks and if the text succeeds it is not in spite of the lack of answers but as a result of that lack. I do not mean by this that I have attempted to be clever; there is no meaning that I am attempting to obscure. Even the most casual fan of the novel will readily recognize allusive moments; I have made no effort to hide them. Flashes of memory gleaned from the novel are fleshed out in *Watches* in ways meant not to disguise what they owe to the novel but rather to make explicit their allegiance. My intention, irrelevant as it is, has always been and remains nothing more than to participate in the generation of the novel's (many) meaning(s) rather than lessen the novel with the stifling proclamation of individual answers.

In the pieces chosen for inclusion here you will perhaps recognize from your own wanderings some innocuous backdrops and props that have come just a bit more to life. But it is my hope that beyond simply bringing elements of the novel to mind, these short musings and daydreams will dredge up the novel in new ways. But keep in mind, dear reader, that while dredging will most certainly bring to surface things heretofore unpredictable, anything that is lifted out leaves behind a larger and deeper hole. –c.p.r.

THE DEIFICATION OF MICHAEL PUIG

"Squash meat gorilla. Mouth tooth. Cry sharp-noise loud.
Bad think-trouble look-face. Cut/neck lip (girl) hole."
—Michael

Michael Puig was born on March 17, 1973 in the western lowlands of
Cameroon. He died of sudden heart failure at the age of 27, a predisposition
for cardiomyopathy being not uncommon.

Red red.

At the time of his death Michael possessed a vocabulary of over 600 lexemes.
Some skeptics argue that Michael never truly used language, the difficulty
being with the asking of questions.

Why do you trouble quiet?

The Archangel, depicted often with large feathered wings and full armor, asks,
"Quis ut Deus?"

Gorilla me Mike.

Jimi Hendrix, Janis Joplin, Jim Morrison, Kurt Cobain, and also Pope John
XII.

Cry sad cry eat red.

Hanno the Carthaginian encountered a savage people in 500 B.C. Later,
American missionary Thomas Savage obtained the first specimens in the form
of skulls and other bones.

More gorilla chase.

The word relic, from the Latin *reliquaie* meaning "remains" or "something left behind," being some portion of the physical[1] remains of a saint or venerated person.

Trouble think pull-out-hair.

And Joseph Merrick, who could not sleep lying down due to the weight of his head, who died attempting to sleep lying down, who may have suffered, from a dislocation of the spine, from Proteus Syndrome.

Quiet sorry quiet good.

"Theory of mind is the ability to attribute mental states—beliefs, intents, desires, pretending, knowledge, etc.—to oneself and others and to understand that others have beliefs, desires, and intentions that are different from one's own."

Michael played music on strings held taut between fingers and toes, was a passionate and talented painter whose work has been exhibited to international acclaim, loved yellow.

"Theory of mind is a theory insofar as the mind is not directly observable."

Posthumous study of Michael's anterior cingulate and fronto-insular cortexes revealed an abundance – comparable to that found in some humans – of large spindle-shaped neurons. Such neurons have been known to appear in humans and, more sparsely, in great apes. And whales. And, at three times greater concentration, in elephants.

---

[1] My father's hands, being both large in span and also thick of flesh, turn and turn, press the table and lift the air while he watches. He might be bringing an aroma slowly to his face, but he is only speaking. My father's hands were massive, he says. Much bigger than mine, he says. My father's hands are massive, much bigger than mine. I inspect the nubs at the ends of my arms, the spindly fingers, the impossible shortness of my reach. I fail to see the dinner plates they will become. Like paws, he says. I am dismayed at the withering of generations.

Michael, who remembered the death of his mother.

Buddha's tooth, the holy foreskin, and seven heads of St. John the Baptist being other relics of note.

And Nebuchadnezzar, who dreamed a huge tree, suddenly cut.[2]

Big-trouble do.

Daniel 12:1.

Me gorilla good thief smile trouble.

And Robert Leroy Johnson, who may have made a deal.

---

[2] sempiternal. That means it goes on forever, unchanging. Set here in text, it stands like a tree planted paper-thin, year after year, never stepping in any direction, silent. Static. The text says nothing but elicits its words from the outside, sees a self intended in the attending mouths of its environs. Existing within and without. Ventriloquist venture. Such is the sense of the unspoken text. And as some somebody says, "In this preliminary remark and these concrete illustrations, I only wish to point out that you and I are always already subjects, and as such constantly practice the rituals of ideological recognition, which guarantee for us that we are indeed concrete, individual, distinguishable and (naturally) irreplaceable subjects. The writing I am currently executing and the reading you are currently performing are also in this respect rituals of ideological recognition, including the 'obviousness' with which the 'truth' or 'error' of my reflections may impose itself on you." But of course what this doesn't allow for is the impossible likelihood that in fact it is all true, all error, and neither fact precludes nonsense. And through it all, the text remains, unchanging Proteus, standing ready to be rebuilt, reread in the image of its incompleteness, to revel in the lives it will one day come to have lived. And if it remembers anything of its earlier versionings, what would that signify to the next? Sempervirens. It goes on changing forever, a continually reset text, reaching higher, spreading roots six feet deep. Sheathed in sheets of paper each year, another ring older. Unchanging evergreen. Millenial watcher. Metasequoia. Cryptomeria. Clinging to the spinning world, waiting to let go. What does it know? The timbre of timber tipped, tampered tamber. Like earth slowly sundered. A pitless pitiless apricot split and heard, by the tiniest ear; such is the sound of the falling giant soon to be mouldered by microbes. A receding wave that serves to curve the impending crash. Bacterial turnaround bringing about a sprouting, composing a new whole from its own disintegration. All of which is to suggest a text not eternal exactly, but

Devil me show you.

And Jean-Michel Basquiat, who was a painter too.

Red sorry quiet good.

And Daniel, who read the writing on the wall, may be buried in Babylon, Kirkuk, Muqdadiyah, Susa, Malamir, and Samarkand.

And Michael appreciated Luciano Pavarotti, who died at the age of 72. As did Louis Althusser.

Michael's heart broke, the problem being a predisposition for sensitivity. His adoptive sister, told that Michael had become an angel, responded only, "Imagine."

The Archangel defeated the dragon, asking, "Quis et Deus?"

Me, Myself, Good.[3]

---

[3] For a compelling interpretation of Michael's place in the novel, the editors recommend Belgian duo Ronny & Renzo's "Me, Myself, Good" from King Kung Foo Records.

WHALE FALL[1]

My little sister was born. I was 7. Dad took me from school, gave cigars to my uncles. I picked her name, Violet. Watching her breathe her first baby breath. And scream. I don't have a little sister, never did.

That's what it's like, not as simple as knowing.

Violets. Baby's breath. Amaryllis. Chrysanthemum. Delphinium. Dahlia. Dandelion. Gardenia. Peonies. Wisteria. Himawari. Sakura. And scream.

I stood in the crib, not my crib, waited for someone to find me. In the morning, waiting for someone, at the house in Gardena, the one with those little stones in the backyard, star-shaped like sembei. And the next-door neighbors who couldn't come out to play after their parents saw our faces. And the dog with the small name that bit me.

There's no scar. That's what it's like, never quite sure if it's really a windmill.

I live in a skull.

I fly a four-chambered heart, held by a baleen string.

---

[1] Despite the many widely noted allusions the following piece appears to make to the band by the same name and its self-titled debut album, Rosenthal has steadfastly maintained his ignorance of the band's existence at the time of its first writing. On the subject of the reading public's insistence that there must in fact be some connection between them, Rosenthal allows, in the Fall 2014 issue of Parthenogenesis that "…they are not wrong. Because they see them, the connections are there. It's news to me, but that's hardly relevant."

In the fall the leaves on the Japanese maple out front catch fire, fall by November. The redwoods stand in tight circles and cut their eyes sideways without comment. In the spring the seedlings peek from beneath the ground smelling of tiny superlatives.

I swallow sound.

She was sitting on the commode when I walked into the bedroom. I thought I wasn't supposed to see. She smiled with half her face and beckoned me to sit on her lap. Or I sat on her lap. Or none of this happened.

That's what it's like.

Many years later I saw him again, never having met him before. His red hair had turned silver. His back had bent. He walked ponderously. I called him by name.

At his flat we made stone soup. That's definitely what it's like.

And death. Heart attacks, aneurysms, strokes and degenerative diseases, cancers – lung, bone, colorectal, breast, brain, cervix and prostate, complications from diabetes, once from the flu and once even a severe asthma attack. I was murdered at 33 and went through a windshield when I was 27. But that's what it's like.

Context is irrepressible. And imaginary.

I started the day folding paper cranes and soon dug splayed hands through piles of dry wings, holding out hope for the shell of a tortoise beneath their missing feet. I sneezed and they lost their grip on the ground and a thousand cranes blinked out against the faded sky. In the quiet behind the sound of senbazuru, finally grown still, I settled to the ocean floor and waited for the echoes of lives I never lived.

RHINOCEROS

The sound of the doorbell cut sharp through the apartment. Rhinoceros'
oatmeal spilled. Rhinoceros watched the viscid cereal spread in the places and
piles where it had hit the floor and considered options. Teresa the cleaning
lady wouldn't come again until Thursday. When the doorbell rang a second
time, Rhinoceros lay all asquirm on his side on the kitchen floor, angling his
horn to allow his lips the furthest possible reach into the corner where the last
bit of oatmeal huddled just under the cabinets. Rhinoceros was as startled by
the second ring as by the first. Rhinoceros' head yanked, caught the side of
his mouth on the corner of the cabinet door with the power of unthinking
movement.

"Just a minute!" Rhinoceros tucked his feet beneath him and pressed them
into the floor until he had risen to his full height. The handle of the door
that had attacked Rhinoceros hooked his horn and ripped clear of its hinges.
Rhinoceros lifted a sigh from deep within himself and backed out of the
kitchen with his head down, ears swiveled away from the cabinet door's
clatter as it thrashed to a full stop on the linoleum.

At the door Rhinoceros stood on tiptoe and failed to see out the peephole.
A western black rhinoceros stands four and a half to five and a half feet tall
at the shoulder. Rhinoceros was on the short side. He could raise his head
further, but could accomplish neither the height nor the angle necessary.
Rhinoceros considered a small hop with his front feet before remembering
that a) his eyesight was terrible and b) the inevitable landing would a) be rude
to the downstairs neighbours (parents to an easily triggered infant) and
b) likely cause structural damage he could ill afford to repair.

Rhinoceros heard the man (he could smell that it was a man) holding his
breath. Or he didn't hear the man holding his breath, but he heard no
breathing. Rhinoceros inferred. He spoke through the door.

"May I help you?"

"I have a package here for a—" his sentence paused for reading, "Rhinoceros?"

"Can you put it through the slot?"

"I'm afraid not sir. The slot's too narrow and I need you to sign."

"Okay, well."

"Sir?"

"Yes, I'll open the door it's just, I'm a rhinoceros."

"A rhinoceros Sir?"

"Yes, a rhinoceros. I didn't want you to be startled." Rhinoceros grasped the knob in his lips and swung the door wide. The postman stood in navy blue slacks, blue windbreaker, and beige pith helmet. Rhinoceros didn't know mail carriers still wore pith helmets. Besides a bulky blue canvas bag sprouting the bent edges of envelopes and small parcels, all the postman appeared to possess were a clipboard and a package about the size of a bunch of bananas. Rhinoceros made a mental note to get more bananas.

"Oh, you're a rhinoceros."

"*Diceros bicornis longipes* to be precise."

"I thought maybe you were speaking metaphorically."

"Nope, just a rhinoceros."

"Well Mr. Rhinoceros,"

"No mister. Just Rhinoceros."

"Yes, of course. Well," the postman considered the brown paper wrapped package in his hands.

"You can leave it inside the door there."

The postman pressed one hand against the outer frame and bent his torso forward, kicking one leg out behind him. The package slid to a stop on the floor and the straightened postman held out his clipboard and a pen Rhinoceros hadn't noticed.

"You should bend with the knees." Rhinoceros stepped forward and grasped the pen with his lips. The postman's feet shuffled. His watery smile stiffened. Rhinoceros finished and shifted his lips.

"Thank you." The postman continued looking at Rhinoceros through somewhat narrower eyes. "So, you're sure you're not a metaphor?"

"No, I'm really just a rhinoceros."

"You're sure you're not, like, a hippopotamus or something?"

"Just us odd-toed ungulates in here." Rhinoceros lifted a hind foot and waggled it out to the side, unsure whether it actually reached far enough to be seen around the widest point of his considerable girth from the postman's point in space.

"So, you live by yourself?"

Rhinoceros was feeling ready to be done with this. "Yes, it's just me."

"That's odd. Before you came to the door I could've sworn I heard a crash."

Rhinoceros took a deep breath and pressed it out through his nostrils. He couldn't see the postman well. He raised his head until the tip of his front horn interrupted their eye contact.

"Well, I had better be getting on with my route."

"You have a nice day."

Rhinoceros stared absently at the door, waiting while the water's surface settled. When the ripples had spread beyond the edge of his attention, Rhinoceros turned to the package the postman had left. The return address was too small to read, black marks on a white label, but Rhinoceros could smell, had smelled plainly since before he'd opened the door, that it had come from his mother. He'd spent the first three years of his life by her side; her smell was as familiar to Rhinoceros as was his own even now, so long after he'd left her.

The downstairs neighbors would be putting the baby down for a nap anytime now. Rhinoceros walked gingerly to the window. Once he'd nudged it sufficiently open (difficult at first, but easier after he got it started) Rhinoceros sat, rested his chin on the sill, and closed his eyes. He tried to remember the sound of a wide-open space, but even with the noise of the city arriving unobstructed, Rhinoceros still heard the quiet of the apartment that sat behind him, the edges of its limited expanse.

Back in the kitchen, Rhinoceros nosed open the fridge. Why hadn't he bought more bananas? Rhinoceros put a pot of water to boil and lipped a package of Top Ramen onto the counter. He needed to eat better, but cruciferous vegetables were hard to come by in the neighborhoods where he tended to find himself, and shopping was rarely simple. Rhinoceros tried to minimize contact with people. For the past four months Rhinoceros mostly only interacted with the man who ran the bodega down on the corner. It was a good situation, despite the poor selection of foods suited to an herbivore. Rhinoceros got into the habit of shopping in the small window between night owls and early risers. The man behind the counter had always waited—while Rhinoceros eased around corners and down tight aisles with held breath—engrossed in his newspaper until the counter was full and Rhinoceros stood waiting. When he was finished, the man hung the bags of groceries on Rhinoceros' front horn, not ceremoniously which would have made Rhinoceros feel self-conscious, but with an air of familiarity born of repetition that helped Rhinoceros to feel in some way a part of the community in which he lived. In four months, the man at the bodega had mentioned the fact of Rhinoceros' rhinocity not once and Rhinoceros was happy not to raise the subject himself. The only intrusion the man at the bodega ever made was to ask if Rhinoceros would like to buy a lottery ticket, which Rhinoceros never did.

It was a monotone existence in the city. But Rhinoceros was becoming inured to the inconvenience. When Rhinoceros was preparing to leave his mother, she had told him that his dad had been in the theater. Rhinoceros had come to the city hoping to find him, but in three years he had yet to hear of another urban rhinoceros, thespian or otherwise. The closest he'd come was a handful of people reporting another rhinoceros who looked *a lot like you*, which in every case turned out to have actually been him. Every six months or so Rhinoceros moved to another city with a vibrant theater scene, each time carrying with him whatever remaining hope he had not yet spent.

Rhinoceros wondered often what his dad might be like, and if he'd ever find him. Rhinoceros had to admit that his efforts were becoming more perfunctory and less charged with any real faith in his eventual success. When he'd just started Rhinoceros attended as many plays as his finances allowed. Just a couple months into his stay in New York he had downgraded to mostly just asking around and reading dramatic reviews. It wasn't that he'd given up exactly, but the thrill and mystique of the theater had long since faded for Rhinoceros. The hassle involved with actually getting in to see plays just wasn't worth the (anticipated but so far immaterial) payoff. And half the time they turned him away, saying they were afraid to "disrupt the play." As if any true patron could aim their attention anywhere other than the stage once those lights went down. He once had dreamt of being in the audience and seeing a rhinoceros enter the stage in the late acts of Hamlet or King Lear or Waiting for Godot to twist the plot or save the day or foil a plan, and knowing, just knowing, that that was his dad. He might turn to his neighbor for a sotto voce "that's my dad up there!" And when that play would end, no one would cheer louder. No, Rhinoceros had not given up, but as the months accrued, the faith which had once been so close to Rhinoceros that he didn't even see it as something separate from himself had slowly grown thin and tattered and less substantial so that in order to maintain critical density Rhinoceros had to press it down into a smaller and smaller ball he kept hidden from judgment, including his own, lest it be deemed a lie told only to paint over futility.

Rhinoceros' thoughts turned to his mother. It was getting late in the afternoon. Rhinoceros imagined dusky light, elastic purple shadows bleeding into waning orange. She was probably browsing for food after a late stop at the water.

Something flapped down on the tip of his smaller horn. Rhinoceros yanked back into his body, opened his eyes to see two birds, no, he was cross-eyed, one bird, brown with red bill and yellow rings 'round the eyes, staring in short bursts from the changing angles offered by a fidgety avian neck. He had never seen one of these in the city before. The bird was only beginning to strike Rhinoceros as implausible when it held forth with a trilling hiss and burst into a thwapping of wings. He heard its wings against the air and each other long after it left him.

Rhinoceros smelled the smoke. The flames licked up the wall of the kitchen behind a black lump on the stove glowing red at the edges that had recently been his favorite pot. The smell of ruined metal scoured his sinuses. Something popped loudly and the flames jumped higher and wider in the small apartment.

Rhinoceros jumped and spun in the air. He didn't know he could do that. He dashed through the closed door and slammed with all his weight into the wall across the hall. He charged, unhindered by the grabbing of the walls, leaving behind him the gaping spaces of impact.

Rhinoceros was the first one out of the building, but it wasn't long before a crowd began to gather around the burning. Fire engines came and tiny men on long ladders sprayed elephantine steaming streams down on the blaze. Men and women sat wrapped in blue blankets in the back doors of ambulances Rhinoceros had not noticed arriving. The firefighters didn't fight the fire so much as guide it vigilantly while it glutted itself to exhaustion. The arc of men in heavy coats expanded and contracted like a crowd of schoolchildren cheering an ill-advised fight between classmates. The angular frame of flames collapsed into glowing coals then smoldering embers then mucky ash, and night fell. All around him in the crowd Rhinoceros heard people wondering what had happened.

The memory of heat from the recently blazing fire indicated a chill in the air. The late summer nights were growing crisp. Winter was coming. Rhinoceros wondered what the weather was like in Los Angeles.

ELEPHANT STORY

I am not an elephant. My definitive characteristic as an individual is that I am not pink. There are seven women, including me, and at the moment eleven children. I'm the only one with grey skin. It's the reason I'm still alive.

My mom was grey. My father was a pig, though I never knew him. Before Mom died she told me as much as she knew. She asked me to remember.

When there were elephants, they were all grey and they were all giants. It's hard to remember exactly, small as I was, but my mom was giant, much taller than I am now. She was an elephant after all. I barely reached her knee when I stood, and her trunk reached nearly twice around me at my middle. Her trunk was so long.

I'm not that tall, not like an elephant, though I'm taller than the others. My trunk is shorter than an elephant's, more blunt, more clumsy. My legs are shorter too. My feet don't hear as well and my ears are much smaller. But my skin is grey like my mom's and that makes me stand out.

Not that it matters. Almost no one will choose me. And if they did, they wouldn't get me. I look like I'm on the menu, but I'm not.

There was a time when people came just to look at the other animals. Everyone lived until they died of natural causes. I don't know this, but my mom remembered it. She was the oldest daughter of the oldest mother. I'm the oldest now and now I remember for her. There was a time when the people pointed and it meant nothing.

Now there are no elephants. Everyone crowds the ground with their heads down, sweeping their trunks in the dust. And when the people point— nobody comes just to look anymore.

I've been pointed to seven times. Each time the people who pointed jabbed their little finger things—*yes, that one, the grey one*—their tiny eyes wide and round, and I smelled their hunger, so sour, aimed at me.

Each time people point at me, someone else dies. It's not my fault. I know it's not my fault. It's the skin, yes, but really it's that no one remembers elephants anymore. I'm not that much taller than the others, but it's enough. I remind them of the elephants they don't remember. If they remembered they'd see how small I am, how meager. But because they don't remember, they see grey skin and draw me larger in their empty frames. I'm just convenient. It's not my fault.

A person points, someone dies. That's how it works.

The people didn't stop eating the other animals, they only forgot it was what they'd always done. They cut them into little pieces and changed their names. They forgot so well that when people stopped coming to the zoo, eating animals seemed like a new idea.

It's not as if nobody ever ate an elephant before people started doing it. An organized party of lions could do it. And there were, as Mom used to say, *those damn hyenas.* Even vultures. *But that was different. Out there it was sad, but it was an understandable thing. This is not that.*

No one understood at first. The smell of new and unfamiliar animals is not so unusual at a zoo. The sound of animals coming to terms with an enclosed space is compelling for those of us born here but is not in itself unexpected. But soon enough it became clear the new additions to the community were something different. This is hard for me to explain. Their difference is something that has never existed for me, being what I am. All of us being what we are. How can I remember it as my mother did? I can't.

The elephants never saw the pigs, though they heard them. And smelled them—the redolence of resignation, born of generations of debasement and self-awareness. That stench – thick, cloying, rotten – was what let the elephants know that something new and wrong was coming to them.

A typical elephant bears a child and raises it to independence and then bears another child. This is how time worked. A typical elephant never existed in a zoo. My mother gave birth only once after she came to the zoo and before she had me. A stillbirth. *I followed her smell after they took her. I smelled her breaking apart. I smelled her in pieces all around me. I couldn't understand. I still smelled her when they dug up her bones and brought them back together. After that they took her further away until I smelled nothing on the air but the memory of her death.* She told me the story only once but I remember it well. It became the story of her death too. I couldn't understand it either.

Elephants counted generations. That was the way through time. That was the story they told. It had no beginning. It just kept going in either direction. It went back as far into the night as I could keep her awake to tell.

I'm very old now. My grey skin is thin and loose. I'm not sick but I am not well. Slippery drips from the tip of my trunk drop dark craters in the dust. Breathing is labor. It all hurts. I've given birth three hundred and forty-seven times. Three hundred and forty-seven times I've smelled the death of my flesh. The screams of three hundred forty-seven deaths have run up my legs and lodged themselves inside me. None of my children have lived long enough to be told the story of generations. It isn't their story anyway; we aren't elephants anymore.

We aren't the only ones that have been changed. They brought chickens to the flamingo, cows to the hippopotamus and rhinoceros. They've done other things I can't quite name, strange things that smell like nothing we remember.

I remember and expect understanding.

Pungent, like warm rotting grasses. A smell that catches in my stubby trunk, leaves a residue I still smell after it ends. Or it might be that it doesn't end. Acrid like steam lifting off an open body. We all have it. No one seems to notice anymore.

I won't give birth again. My body is exhausted. Already I've birthed far more than any elephant ever did. They gave up trying to pull more from me after the fifth dead baby came out with pink skin going already grey. Not grey like me, but grey like death, like deflated lungs, like depleted resources. Time stopped. A shiny mass of pink and dead, bulbous and leggy, hardly formed, fallen heavy and limp to the ground like a slippery hot organ.

Was my mother really so tall? Was her trunk really so long?

The story that stretches back without beginning, I remember. Like land reaching out in every direction as far as sound travels through ground. Towering crowds of wrinkled grey skin, long articulate trunks embraced in rolling knots, mothers and sisters, children hidden at the center of so many thick legs, a barrier of elephants. Mom remembered. Fighting lions to a standstill. Swimming in water deeper than daylight. Walking for days in a straight line. I remember for her.

And if elephants never existed? If my grey skin is no remnant of distant history but rather a random mistake? What then is all that I remember? What do I know?

I know the smell of dead elephants on the breath of the people who crowd around to watch us wander nowhere. I know they come to point and choose. They laugh and spit bits of skin and bone, pick their teeth with twiggy fingers, go home with elephant ear hats and full stomachs. I know that when I'm dead, and my grey skin no longer signifies, they will break me into small pieces, and burn me slowly in fire, and bury these memories in the ground.

THE MANIFEST

HE WAS ALWAYS stumbling over his arms when he woke in the middle of the night to pee. Already unsteady on sleepy feet feeling fat like a numb tongue, he'd shoot his hands out ahead of himself as he pitched forward, his kicked limbs skittering across the floor, crashing into standing lamps or wrapping around table legs or finding the wall with the sound of meat and bone, slapping and knocking in a quick series of articulate impacts. Except he had no hands to shoot. It was only after he'd finished falling all the way to the floor that he'd wake enough to know his arms were nowhere.

I believed in the therapeutic potential of the technology. The tech wasn't the problem. That part was relatively simple once we managed a reliable deployment mechanism for the opposing active properties of the two proteins – adducin and musashi.

Miyamoto Musashi was born sometime in the late 16th Century. An early biography suggests 1584, the year of the monkey, the twelfth year of the Tensho era, a date procured by counting backwards from *Gorin no Sho*, a text many times translated from 17th-Century Japanese, in which Musashi states that he is "age sixty." According to the Miyamoto family's koseki, Musashi was born in 1582 when koseki were already a ten centuries old tradition.

Japanese law requires the reportage of births, deaths, marriages, divorces, adoptions, disruptions, and paternity to local authorities for the maintenance of koseki. Some events are legally recognized only after they are recorded in the koseki. Births and deaths are exceptions and are legally allowed to have happened as soon as they happen. Musashi may have been born to Munisai's first or second wife or adopted from another family. His mother likely died in childbirth, or was divorced by Musashi's father and left the boy behind, or took him with her and remarried, or was someone else entirely. The tomb of Munisai – Musashi's father – was born in 1580.

In his dreams, his arms multiplied, proliferating around him as fast as his gaze could sweep, as far as it could see, akimbo in every direction. The valley floor was the bottom of a bowl bloody full of limb salad. They couldn't all be his. But who would know, if he took just two? One right and one left was all he needed. But standing was so hard, with so many arms and legs draping dead weight like the limbs of sleeping bedfellows. His toes caught on crooks of elbows. A foot pressed against the wrong side of a knee joint, a shifting tibia, a pile of pick up sticks ready to collapse. And anyway how could he carry them?

We had not an overabundance of foresight, but we knew at least that we'd need some control, a reference, a master against which to monitor deviations. First it was interviews with the subjects themselves, then each member of each subject's squad, followed by squad leaders, friends and family from home, former supervisors from part-time jobs, teachers, neighbors, long lost childhood friends, ex-boyfriends and girlfriends and allies and bullies and other relevant classmates, hometown merchants and businesspeople, summer camp dalliances, pen pals and landlords and property managers, coaches, neighborhood kids who mowed lawns or raked leaves or ran the adjacent sidewalks, a handful of operators standing by to assist you, as many mail carriers as had worked all relevant routes at relevant times, and the odd gardener.

Musashi's childhood name was Bennosuke. And it was Shinmen Takezo. His Buddhist name was Niten Doraku, but nobody remembers him that way; Niten Doraku is no samurai name. Takezo was born in Miyamoto Village.

Later, he spent three years in a closed room reading by the light of an oil lamp. The monk who put him there called it a womb, a room with the blood of his ancestors staining the doors and beams black like lacquer. Takezo was reborn through reading. Musashi is an alternate reading of the same characters that write Takezo. Some of this definitely probably happened.

All subjects were compelled to keep journals from the time they were identified for the project. We told them the journals were private, a safety valve to help them cope with the stress of their symptoms and engage with the process of recovery. We carried flashlights and pens into their rooms while they slept, copying down the gist of things they'd kept to themselves.

Musashi might have been at the Battle of Sekigahara on the twenty-first day of October in the year 1600. He might have fought for the losing side in a battle that would lead to long years of peace following long years of civil war. He might have woken on the fifteenth day of the ninth month of the fifth year of the Keicho era, adrift in a sea of corpses, barely alive.

The way he looked at them on the ground and they were just things. He meant to pick them up, get them off the ground quickly. Three-second rule. He meant to take them away to a safe place where he might set about reattaching. The members of his squad within earshot when it happened agreed; it was the sound of a very large drumstick tearing from a very large raw chicken. He meant to pick them up, but couldn't begin. He only stood over them looking until he passed out. All of them said drumstick, suggesting poultry. None of them said leg. Which wouldn't have made sense either.

Regular ongoing interviews were recorded and crosschecked. Elisions were often identified quite easily. Among them an unfortunate birthday party, a childhood pet, a knack for guitar, a love of dancing, three first sexual encounters – each of them objectively awkward, several previous addresses, *Robinson Crusoe*, a divorce, one of two identical twin childhood friends, seven individual primary reasons for enlisting, quadratic equations, kenophobia, mythophobia, nomatophobia, nostophobia, hippophobia, and how to work a manual transmission. Some were not so easily quantified. The texture of burlap, the taste of oatmeal, the smell of burning hair, and blacktop the day after rain, the two bits for a shave and a haircut, the color red, the end of *The Mystery of Edwin Drood*, the difference between ophthalmologists and optometrists, that scene in *The Wizard of Oz* with Dorothy and the pig pen, the animal identity of a favorite childhood stuffed toy named Edgar, the appropriate number of glasses of water a day to drink, the letter Q, and how to do taxes.

More than a hundred thousand remain officially missing in action. Which might mean dead, but doesn't. Missing in action is the sharp intake of breath before speaking. It's the

We tried targeting different regions of the brain, but it never turned out quite how we imagined. One subject stopped sneezing or coughing, forgot (how) to swallow, and finally stopped breathing independent of external manipulation. Another we were forced to wake with negative olfactory stimuli. First we used spoiled food, then feces, and finally rotting offal, until that too lost its effect. We hoped to remove another subject's obsolete memory of the body's pre-injury weight distribution. The only recorded result was a distinct worsening of posture. We thought we might dampen another subject's nociceptive distress but instead disrupted the somatosensory processes and were forced to remove all furniture from the subject's room. Another stopped moving altogether.

We weren't discouraged. We called it due diligence, exploring all avenues of therapeutic possibility, but already the haphazard dash forward and the treatment of subjects as a renewable resource had begun to feel less like science, more like falling.

If you understand, things are just as they are; if you do not understand, things are just as they are.

Eventually we made our way to the hippocampus. The memories we were after were always already there.

Musashi developed a style of wielding two swords simultaneously. Though samurai regularly wore two swords, and most had two hands (at least initially), no one had picked up a second sword before Musashi escaped with his life from the Yoshioka School who were angry with him for having dueled and defeated their master's successor, whose predecessor Musashi had also defeated. Faced with so many enemies' anger, Musashi defeated the successor to the successor to the master of the Yoshioka School. The Yoshioka School ceased to exist while Musashi survived. Maybe.

The subjects' accounts of themselves grew fragile. Their stories became broken backstitches. Larger pieces broke loose and floated away like the arctic ice sheets no one thought would go, damning polar bears and penguins to float on fragments in a stretch of blue where they couldn't make sense. Subjects grew docile, acquiescent, confused and no more fit for return to service than before we'd begun.

It had been a living room. He was there the day before. The day before his first procedure, he cut a thin red line up the inside of his forearm. We were watching; we were able to stop him before he got to the other arm. A red flag had been added to his file. It was something we'd read by flashlight. He was there the day before when it had been a living room. He didn't tell us. The living room had a family, and a friend, and he was there. And we read by flashlight – red on the walls, drying thick and dark in the heat, no longer a living room. We stitched his arm.

We thought we could put them back together. We thought that was what we were doing all along.

He said he hadn't been hurt. He insisted. Not a single wound. But his squad woke the next day to find the latrine floor well-covered with spilled glass, glittering red streaks leaping, red Rorschachs filling empty frames where mirrors had hung. Standing at attention, back straight and chest out, eyes respectfully trained on nothing, red still dripping from his knuckles and oozing from his feet, he insisted he was unharmed, had no idea what had happened.

The instant you speak about a thing, you miss the mark.

It fell to me to catalogue and store collateral extractions. I became curator of leftovers. We kept everything we cut out of them, good and bad. I decided which was which.

His aim was true. It had been a good thing. He had been praised for it, had won rank. He was due for redeployment; he only wanted to stay sharp he said. Clusters of flowers and candles and stuffed animals and crosses had scattered across Washington Square Park. He was convinced he was to receive a medal for bravery. It had been a good thing, he said.

First, she burst into tears. Before that she loosed her grip. Before that the flower fell. After, Musashi picked up the severed stem. The flower was never meant for Musashi, had passed through several sets of hands on its way, illegible to other eyes. He offered her cakes to make amends. Yoshioka Denshichiro dismissed the peony, not even noticing. Later, Musashi brought his bokken down on the shoulder of Seijuro. I don't know what kind of cakes. Red bean? Custard? I never read it in the original Japanese so I don't know. They were only cakes. After, Seijuro begged to have his arm cut off. Before he was obliged it hung like a sack of gravel.

Though the implants dissipated completely and without fail, they appeared to leave ripples in the hosting memory, as with a stone disappeared beneath the water's surface.

His nephew, intending to leap into his uncle's arms as he had always done and expecting only the first half of gravity's rainbow, crashed instead into knees and onto floor. His uncle's sleeves hung, listless trunks of cloth and air.

We never, and probably this is where I should have begun, returned a single soldier to active combat. We lost access to new subjects. The money disappeared. Of course there was no official word before they arrived to take everything. Nobody bothered to threaten us; we'd all understood the situation before we'd begun.

The procedure was over quickly, but it was not painless. She had expected an ending after that. She'd already been transferred. Her CO offered that for her silence. But the baby had still been made, if not born.

It was a risk, sure. But I couldn't let it all be forgotten. The media coverage was scrubbed, spun. War is big business.

He was always stumbling and unfamiliar, no hands to shoot.

So I took them. All that was left were the most traumatic we'd managed to extract, catastrophic bodily injury, slow death, moral incertitude, the absurd impossibility of choice. Absconding was easy enough. I was the only one keeping track. I took the memory of war with me.

Akimbo in every direction, but who would know?

He meant to pick them up, which wouldn't have made sense either.

Don't look for me. You're asking the wrong questions for my answers.
I can't remember you.

Things are just as they are, which might mean dead but doesn't.

Why do I carry these memories with me? For whom? Are they even viable for implantation anymore? And if they are? Will I remember and annihilate them in a flash of euphoria? To accomplish what? What I had hoped to preserve is already irretrievable, traces of something long since gone. These memories are starlight.

The instant you speak is illegible to other eyes.

After nearly a thousand pages, we find Musashi floating toward Funashima, carving an oversized bokken from a broken oar. He rolls sheets of paper, twists them end to end, uses the cord to tie his sleeves. "To Musashi's eyes, life and death seemed like so much froth. When every pore of his body, as well as his mind, forgot, there would remain nothing inside his being but the water and the clouds."

I don't know what kind of cakes.

When Sasaki Kojiro draws his sword, the Drying Pole, The Soul Polisher, he throws his scabbard into the surf.

"You've lost, Kojiro."

She had expected an ending after that.

Sasaki Kojiro, also known as Ganryu.

"Words! Nonsense!"

The instant is born of misreading.

If you understand things, you miss the mark.

Ganryu is still smiling when the broken oar shatters his skull, thinking he has won. "Was it not because man had a fixed, determined form that he cannot possess eternal life? Does not true life begin only when tangible form has been lost?" Perhaps smiling still when Funashima is renamed for him. It is the last time Musashi kills. Maybe.

He rolls sheets of paper in a thin red line, writing Rorshachs in the instant you speak.

"Musashi was watching a small cloud in the sky. As he did, his soul returned to his body, and it became possible for him to distinguish between the cloud and himself, between his body and the universe."

She had expected an ending.

"The world is always full of the sound of waves."

He was always a numb tongue of articulate impacts.

AFTERWORD

THE FIRST WORDS, each time _____ began again, always made
_____ uneasy. Or almost. _____ had read them so many times before that
everything _____ felt about it all, everything _____ had felt about it all
those other times came back to _____ from wherever it was that such a
complex surplus of emotion could hide itself in _____, as an uncanny flock
of birds, all at rest in one tree planted somewhere _____ had never been.
Many times before, as _____ had read those first words _____ had thought
to ___self that _____ might go back, just after, to read them again before
going on, that _____ might in fact read only those first words several times
over before going on to read the rest of the first page even, let alone the
first chapter or anything at all resembling the end of the book, so that the
flood of the initial bursting might radiate longer while _____ went along
through the rest. But every time, as _____ had gotten to the end of those
first words, feeling the rising surface tension of the familiar emotions pressing
out from inside, _____ had just gone on. The next words, you see, strung
the feeling out ahead of _____, not leaving it quite the same, but not quite
leaving _____ either, far enough from the center of _____'s attention not to
overwhelm completely, but near enough not to overwhelm not at all.

Yes, of starlings probably, _____ thought. Those were the ones, weren't they?

That came together in those enormous swarms of more than a million of themselves, all flying in a sort of loose unison that resulted not in an eternal straight line of birds, but rather a roiling cloud of everyone doing something together while simultaneously doing something utterly individually specific? Yes, yes they were. Of starlings then, a murmuration. An overwhelming. The unvoiced syllables of lips whispering. _____ thought the soft sound of such a thing was just right for reading the rest of the words, allowing for enough quiet attention to catch in turn the eye of each bird, to whisper it carefully down from the sky and to swallow it. To go on like that, till each of more than a million birds was at rest in that tree growing somewhere inside _____ after _____ had read the last. And so _____ had always gone on after the last of the first words, rather than backing up to the first of the first words, finding in ___self suddenly the patience for the slowly wonderful work that lay ahead, for truly, _____ had to admit, every time _____ read those first words, _____ did in fact go on to the last.

_____ thought that more than a million is really a lot of birds to carry around in a tree planted somewhere you've never even been because really how could you? You were never there; when would you have picked it up in the first place? And could you really walk around carrying a whole tree without brushing it against the tops of the doorways when you went from room to room, or if you were outside, getting yourself tipped over in the wind, in either case inadvertently flinging any number of that million many starlings into the air about you? But somehow it worked. The starlings stayed settled, all million many of them, and _____ felt certain they'd stay that way until the next time _____ read those first words again, to send them all up again, to swallow them back down again. Whenever _____ got to the last words, the last word, murmured the last bird down into palm to share a last moment of silence before swallowing saying goodbye-for-now, _____ felt certain.

And in that certainty I was, at last, able to find a perch for myself amongst a million more of me. The sound of settling wings, punctuated by tiny eruptions of readjustment, like shuffled papers folding inward, like a million last chuffs of air to clear the throat, called and recalled. Settled. My mind fallen at last to the ocean floor, flight now nothing more than a theory, I couldn't quite recall why all the flutter. I asked around, but I didn't know either. And neither did I. Nor I. Nor any of the rest of me. We suspected we were waiting for something.

Didn't we? We suspected there was something we were meant to do, something we meant to do, something to do, something we meant, you and I, but we couldn't be sure. After words it was hard to say, you said. You said, after words. After words, you said nothing. We go on waiting nonetheless.

APPENDIX A

INSTRUCTIONS

1. CUT THE PAGES following these instructions into strips. 1. Cut the pages following these instructions into strips using the lines of printed text as guides. 1. Cut the pages following these instructions into lines. 1. Beginning with the first page following these instructions, cut the first fifty-two lines. 5. Glue line 52 upside down and back to back with line 1. 5. Again, that's back to back, so as to make the text of each line face away from the other. 5. Legibility is key. 8. If you have made no mistakes thus far, glue line 51 upside down and back to back with line 2. 8. If you have made mistakes, buy a new copy of *Remembering Dismembrance: A Critical Compendium*. Turn to the page titled "INSTRUCTIONS." Return to step 1. 9. Repeat this process, making no mistakes, until the last lines are glued. 10. Glue the end of line 1 to the beginning of line 2. 10. Glue the end of line 1 to the beginning of line 2, accounting for textual orientation. 10. Make no mistakes. 13. Continue in this manner until the end of line 25 has been glued to the beginning of line 26. 10. Alternatively, glue the end of line 27 to the beginning of line 28, accounting for orientation. 11. The daring reader may attempt to glue lines end to end, proceeding numerically. 16. If you find yourself with only one line left, do not despair. 16. If you find yourself with only two lines left, do not despair. 18. Lay flat however many lines you have. 19. Hold one or two ends in each hand, as appropriate

for the number of lines you have. 20. Bring the ends together, so as to make an inside and an outside. 20. Like a rubber band. 22. Insert one half-twist. 23. Without error, glue the ends, however many there are, together. 24. Return to step 1. 24. Return to step 1, substituting lines 1 through 52 for lines 1 through 52. 24. Return to step one, substituting lines 1 through 52 for lines 1 through 52, stopping before step 17. 27. Link the line in hand with any and each existing line already glued. 28. Proceed with step 17. 29. Return to step 1. 30. Continue in this manner until the pages following these instructions have become six interlocking and unending one-sided pages. 30. Continue in this manner until the pages following these instructions have become six inseparable lines. 31. Read at leisure, but always out loud, *accelerando.*

, but if it's broken is it no longer meaningly what it was? Is a broken thing a no thing at all? Is the breaking a bad? A bad thing a thing? Must a thing be broken be fixed? If it's bread? Is the breaking then bad? Being bread broken is sustenance shared. Or an old habit that's hard to. Like a notion and its hold on you that you just can't quite. And some would say that rules are made to be. A mirror maybe won't quite do the thing you thought you wanted, when it's broken, but it will still reflect. Though it probably won't think. The image is troubled, the meaning multiplied by shards, faces fanned out in slices of eyes and nose and half-mouths and more teeth than perhaps you expected. A mirror broken becomes a knifed vision. But a vision split will still be seen, even as scene in pieces. And things that break, but not to pieces? Say sad hearts, heavy spirits (not liquor), wild horses, high fevers and heat waves, old records (though not, in this nonsense, the musical kind), codes, cold fronts, molds, and hard cases – though I suppose those are cracked more than broken, or an egg, which must be cracked open before its yolk can be broken. Then there's the news, which is breaking if it's only just, or can be broken to if it's bad. Being broken is a bit more complicated than it might seem to seem. It's no simple matter of swinging a sledgehammer, and won't always do just to drop a thing from a very great height, like, say, for instance, a promise. Or a bad cycle. Or a vicious one. And then there's the proverbial leg, invoked in the theater to break it don't break it. Name a thing, say it, speak it, avoid it. Not all breaking is bad, nor even dismemberment thus needing rememberment. But dwelling in abstract doesn't do away with the fact that much breaking is indeed an unwanted thing. Hearts and spirits sure, but what of the body? I fell once from a tree and broke both my wrists in one go. My hands hung limply from the ends of my forearms, remembering an unpleasant dream I once had.

Unless those broken wrists and limp hands were the dream. Hard to say for say for. Because even if breaking is real, it's not necessarily touchably touchable, is it? Imagine if I were to stop (don't worry, I won't, I won't and I can't), hold myself still (can't imagine how I would and I won't and I won't). Would that then be motion broken? And if I move again, if I begin to break dance, what's been broken? If it's with words as the weapon then it's silence that's sliced. And what of a complex machine, a computer, that ceases to ceases to properly? We call it broken, but has something snapped or torn asunder? Or is it only a little one somewhere that's tripped into zero? And if I consider a machine even more so, like a mind, any one will do, what then? How many ones to zeroes and back again might it take to make a psychotic? And when it's been achieved, what exactly is it that's been? And if it's avoided, what's saved? And if my savings are none and I fail to play my part of the bill, am I broke? And if I can kill am I morally bankrupt instead? Or if I am merely defeated, bowed under weight of the failings I fail to fail and irrational fears? A broken spirit, which brings to mind a broken spirit, a tamed horse, or a broken mind. This word, this notion, to break, am broke, broken, breaking, a break. With reality? You might call that losing touch, but if I've only grown tired of incessant demanding reality and simply want to take to a break to a break, not break my lease on this life altogether? Is that so bad? What if I promise to promise to come back again? Or what if maybe I only want to break free (like Queen), break up (hard to do), break down (and out), break through (to the other side), break off (no, not that), or at least break even or into. So slippery, this understanding, misunderstanding, like wet soap, slip, like a center of balance off balance just so, or not quite, and in the attempt to break the ice, slip, and broken tailbones. And the bones of tales told, forgotten and so broken, the

tales I mean. If this language will let me mean anything at all. Broken tales, stories

trying to be told. Failing. Narratives snapped or wound up, coiled and sprung. Myths

called up to protect, like prayers along a rosary. But if the beads get loose, if the string is

unstrung, interrupted, the loop no longer, can it still offer absolution? Or does it then

become a curse, a curse needing to be broken again? Again? A simple circle, it holds

meaning in or out or it only is what it is at all times all along that fine line, that story's arc

but there aren't ever only two things, are there? There isn't only the thing and the reflection of the thing. There's the mirror, the pivot, the thing between things, the membrane, the thing that creates the thing, or rather the thing that creates the reflection. Which is it now? Now it is which? So three things, the mirror, the reflection, and the reflection's thing. Though really there's a lot more than just those. Picasso anyone? Look at a thing, now move, now look again, now move, now look. You move, the thing doesn't, but both of you change. A mirror, though, is a different kind of a thing. Face a mirror, look at it, see you, but not you. Move, look again, see something else altogether. Altogether else, something see, again, look, move. You can manage not only to see the mirror thing from another perspective, but you've also enacted a whole new reflection of whatever else the mirror sees. Whoever else. Someone else altogether. But I have to wonder whether all the reflections a mirror can make of me with me are already there, just waiting to be seen. How many reflections has the mirror made before we've managed to stand in the right spot? Though I only read one line of sight at a time, how many lines might there be, running simultaneously? Simultaneously running, there might be many lines of sight, though at a time I only read one. And when the mirror dreams, does it dream them all at once? I imagine a mirror must have a million thoughts, seeing as much as it does. Standing in between as it does, can it tell the difference amongst the reflections and their things? Given its already multitudinous nature, what happens when a mirror is broken? Does it really bring bad luck bad? A mirror might say already the luck bad's been brought once it's broken. But once it's all in pieces, does each bit of mirror know what the others see? Or do they each go on reading their lines of sight in endless loops alone loops alone endless? Wondering, I go on breaking my mirrors,

mirror my breaking, peering into pieces and saying my prayers, praying my sayings, fingering the beads of the rosary, rising to hoping to piecing that narrative surface back together again. But how can the edges meet edges meet edges, when their lines all get loose, lose resolution and warp and distort and bend and turn in my fingers? The pictures they play all go all grotesque, pull like taffy. Funhouse reflections reflect no fun but obsessions. These pictures opposite me become someone else, someone else's many someones else, other obsessions, others' obsessions. Walking down a one-way hall of mirrors I glimpse bits of bent light as my fever is reflected back to back to back to me. And at the end of the hall, if this hall will let me mean anything at all, there is only another mirror, another hall another hall. I wind my way up to it, the mirror I mean not the hall, if this language will let me mean anything at all, walking slowly over words and wondering who spoke them. I stand at the mirror and I look at the way I've just come, unwound. On the other side. But the other side's not the other side, or the other side I see is on the same side as me. And that's the thing about things such as mirrors is they show you the other side's no side at all. There's only one side to this hall. And through the mirror I can see the no other side at all and find me someone else altogether, walking in the opposite direction. So is my reflection me or not me and which side is which? To tell the difference I try to make difference. I look for reflections of self on my self. I've got so many. Eyelids that meet in the middle of my eye, clip. Two eyes and the illusion of depth, pluck. Two arms and at the end of them hands that match, snap one of each off. Two legs, amputate one and go on hopping, jumping along the line of the hall. But how did I manage that? A real body with no arms can't break off a leg. How did I swing a thing to lop one off? Am I only imagining this body I'm unwinding? Or is it simply a

momentum that's gathered once you get going. You start stripping reflections away from yourself and soon enough you can't stop and soon enough you've cut you all away. And all that's left is dreaming the pieces, each reading a separate line of sight. But none of my pieces knows that they're pieces pretending to be wholes and so there's only ever one piece, though there might be many holes. All sides become one and one side becomes too. One piece and one line. One reflection and its thing. One obsession and its reading,

but it's hard to focus to focus. Jumping back and back between the heat that radiates from my skin in undulating waves to the shrinking cold that sinks my chest and knocks my teeth, it's nearly impossible to keep my attention on the task at the task at hand. I don't know what might've caused it, from whom or what or where I might have caught it, or contracted I'll say since caught sounds like something I pursued, which I don't think it was, is. I was taught to know fever not as reaction, not illness. The fever is not the thing that ails you, it is the thing the thing that cures you, saves you. Some virus, bacteria, fungus, toxin, drug, broken blood clot, tumor, exertion, or indulgence, or again something else, is the root, the cause, the catalyst. The fever is your body's attempt to burn it out, cleanse you. Purification by fire. Of course, intellectual understanding is some cold comfort in the midst of sweating, shivering, jittering, oozing in and out of layers of clothing, floppy blankets and sopped sheets tossed back and forth, flourished like cloaks, wound up and down like clocks. A fever aches, then breaks, then breaks. It is self-destruction, the body's natural chemo. In the midst of my fever I stare at the words, watching them swim back and forth through my vision, losing their meanings like water through fingers. Swimming in letters. When was the last time I drank a drink of water? I can't imagine alcohol. I might burst into flames as the liquid hit my tongue. But a drink of water, what would it do? Evaporate? Hiss into vapor in front of my lips? My mind wanders around into silly scenarios, totally useless. But what is tangible? What can I feel and verify, if anything can be verifiably felt? I grow tired, sluggish, heavy, tired, sluggish, heavy, tired. My joints light up as I move, little pings of white and blue, electric shocks in my elbows and shoulders, knees, hips, knuckles, spine. My head, shall I say that it aches? Very well, there is pain, but what of its character? How to know it?

Does it pulse or pound or shoot or throb or squeeze and cinch or burn or crush or press or pierce? Is it dull or sharp? And where is it to be found, this pulsing pounding shooting twisting turning pain? Does it lie over my scalp? Does it stand erect in my neck? Perhaps it drapes my forehead, peeks in at my temples? Or maybe it spins just behind my eyes, little pinwheels of pain. Does it pull down at the front of my face or clench my teeth and my jaw? Perhaps it is lopsided, localized, or mirrored evenly around a centerline, spreading steadily in directions? Or does it dart about, disdainful of categorizing, evading quantification? So say hard to say. I creep up on an answer then lose the ground I gained, slough off, listless. Or I huddle to myself in my jello-y nauseousness, remembering with weepy nostalgia the simple ignorance of feeling, okay. It is weak and melodramatic. There are no beautiful terrifying dreams, only oxymoronic cold sweat shivering heat. Images don't dance before my eyes, earnestly pregnant, so much as slip away like slick fish mostly dead, flipping and falling free of my grip just before I can understand them. That's what fever is, does, produce the inability to produce, be a citizen, even if only of a solitary society. My bedeviled hypothalamus does what it can to regulate the wilds of my insides, but what it can do is little. It is the nose cut off for spite, discarded, ignored in the face of infection, invasion, the ringing alarm reacting late to stealth and heist. But panicked though it be, inside me, at the level of rhizome, mitochondria, platelet and plasma, out here in my mind it rolls. Forward I think, though I think perhaps back, or maybe both. Either way around the rosary it reads with Sisyphian inevitability both up and down, builds toward nothing, stairs to more stairs, no landing, the wave I've dived under and can't get up. Though really fever is no metaphor at all. Fever is the thought I might vomit, unwanted purge. Dislocated pain

disembodied. Fever is distraction, or focus shifted to the space between a thing and a

thing. Fever is this thick viscous sulfuric water up to my chin. I am only a head left,

feeling the phantom movements of limbs remembered beneath an opaque surface. I try to

move, to move in a meaningful, a way, to step, step, to definitively, in a step, a direction.

I try to speak, clearly to say, what I mean to say. I try to mean, something. If this

language will let me mean anything at all. I try to write a line that lines up and behaves,

and I realize I'm in a freshly dug grave. Except there's further to go and so I pick up the shovel and I'm flinging flings of dirt up and out, and the bottom beneath my feet disappears a bit at a time and this ought to make sense because I'm digging I'm digging I know that I'm digging, but it's wrong like the rate of my digging and the rate of the falling bottom don't quite add up and I look down and I think I see something trying to poke through and I drop the shovel and I get down on my knees and I start to dig with my hands and I try to wipe the dirt away to see what's beneath the dirt beneath the dirt. I want to look back up over my shoulder but am sure I'll see the sky rushing down at me so don't look can't and I dig I dig faster and the words pile up beneath my broken fingernails and I can almost just see what's there beneath the beneath and I dive in my fingers in deep and I press my palms out and open a space to push in with my forehead and in the darkness can almost see but it's so dark and so cold and I realize I'm looking into the freezer and I'm reaching in with my arm to get something but I can't quite see what. I reach in further, stand on my toes, stretch and flinch when my skin hits the ancient walls, covered with burned ice and I still can't quite reach it. I push aside frozen peas, lift and move shiny wrapped meat, heavy and hard like a stone and I can see further now, further back into the freezer. It's darker and vapors swirl across my vision where cold air hits my warm. I lean in further and feel the ceiling of the freezer on the back of my neck, hitch up one leg, get my knee over edge and lurch forward. A little further in, past the ice cube trays filled with tiny mirrors, I can almost reach what it was I was after, which makes me look back and the kitchen looks so far away, like I could never walk all the way back, but I think I see something, someone coming after me and I've got to go further in. Walking over ice, knees bent, palms out on either side to guard my balance, it

grows harder to see where I'm headed as the walls grow close and the furry ice bumps

my ear and I realize I'm talking on the phone. And cold as it is I press the receiver close

against my ear, and I think I must be dreaming, but I can't quite hear what it is that's

being said on the other side. What? I said I can't quite hear what's being said and I think

I must be dreaming and I press the receiver more firmly to the side of my head and I look

down the wound cord and it's got a cord? And I follow it all the way to the phone's body

and I see it's a rotary phone and I didn't even know they make rotary phones anymore

and I still can't quite hear what's on the other side so I listen harder and press the receiver

so hard I feel my skin bulging in through the tiny holes in the plastic cover that covers the

receiver and still I can't hear so I press harder, push in through the holes and inside the

receiver it's dark and I see myself spotted all over by pins of pins of light coming in

through the tiny holes until something covers them from the outside and I can't see at all

and I turn and run deeper into the receiver, hoping to hear what it is that's being said

being said and I can see just a tiny bit of light scattered on the ground and a few steps

further in I trip over some old shoes and I realize I'm in the closet and I'm cleaning

which means it must be must be spring and I'm pushing aside hanging clothes and

pulling boxes and checking the contents and they're all full of old postcards and letters

and there are so many letters and I lift them out in messy sliding piles, using both hands

like shovels and there are so many letters. I want to read them all and I need to read them

all, but I must have read them before. They look familiar don't they? And I keep

shoveling but there are too many letters and they're piling up around me and I see that

my legs have disappeared beneath the growing pile and still I'm digging feverishly with

my shovelhands and the letters are rising like water and I think I might drown but I know

there's no way I'll ever get up and out and anyway there are only more letters coming

down upon letters and so I dive, thinking there must be a drain down at the bottom

somewhere and I swim down through the letters, down with my shovelhands and the

lower I go the darker it gets and I can't quite read the letters as they float by as I dive as it

gets darker the lower I go and I think I see the drain and I feel it with my shovelhands and

I scrape and press down and bits of letters get in my eyes, go gritty in my mouth like dirt

but the vague feeling of déjà vu never leaves me. It's there with me when I go to bed at night. And it's not just that I've gone to bed before, that I know my bed from so many nights gone by. It's more than memory. It's an also knowing. A knowing at the same time that I'm knowing. It's there with me when I wake up in the morning. And it's not just that I've seen the sun come up before, that I know the day from so many already begun. It's not just the day and the night. It's the day and the night. Or that there's only one day and only one night, or one day and night, and no way to tell which is which, or rather what is what. It's the feeling that at any moment I find myself, it might not be the only moment at which I could find myself. It's the feeling that if I could, in any of those moments, flip to the other side of the side of the world, that I might find myself elsewhere altogether, elsewhen, and walking in the opposite direction. It's the thought of walking up behind myself on the sidewalk. That's the problem. My problem. My multiple me's. My quantum existence. I get the faint feeling I'm never quite saying what I'm saying. It's not that I'm saying less. It's not even that I'm saying more. It's that I'm saying what I'm saying also, in addition to, though in addition to what I can't say. Or maybe I can and I have, but I can't quite remember. No, not not remember, that's not it. It's not a matter of having happened before and not now. I can't quite hear myself say it. Or saying it. Yes, that's more like what it is. Einstein was the one, wasn't he, who talked about time and space bending, turning back on itself? Stephen Hawking too, no? Yes? But those are only theories aren't they? Which of course doesn't necessarily mean that they're not in fact accurate, only that they haven't been verified. Yet. Or aren't verifiable. Yet. But what if they were? What if you could hold the world in your hands? What if you could hold it and turn it and look at it from any angle, bend it yourself, bend

yourself? Myself? Or watch it, like a monitor, like a river, but one that can be pushed and pulled and run in either or any direction. What if the world were a tape to be wound, slid back and forth, run through your fingers like a rosary? Grains of sand, which is to say sand, in an hourglass to be flipped. And all those moments to be seen at one go. That's the feeling I get. That's the feeling I get when I walk down the street and wonder where else I might be. That's the feeling I get when I'm missing a place I'm in, a moment I'm at, and a who I am already. It's the little flap of skin on the roof of my mouth that I can't stop tonguing. It's the loose thread I've got to pull. I tongue it, I pull it, but the vague feeling of déjà vu never leaves me. All these analogies, all these pronouns, referents unclear, metaphors not dead, but broken, they fail. Perhaps I can't quite say what it is because it isn't an it, but rather an it and also a that and a this as well, a these or those. All the pronouns, all the referents, not to be encompassed in one speech act, but rather to be spoken with my multivalent, double-sided voice. These are the stories I tell myself while I walk through my days. These are the fictions I slide through my fingers to explain what I can't explain. These are the ways I try to tell my fever dream, a dream I've never actually seen, but get the sense is somewhere just behind me, as if I might glimpse it if I were to look over my shoulder just fast enough. Like trying to turn my head to see my own ear. Like standing before a mirror, except turned inside out. As if I'm always standing back to back to back to my reflection. These are the things I try to forget. But I never can quite. Because even when I forget, there's still the chance that I've not forgotten elsewhere, or rather elsewhen, or elsewhat. I'm not sure the word for it. The other side. The quantum space. There's a quorum of me, but no decorum. And so we can't decide to ignore that flap of skin, that squiggling bit of thread, my reflection

behind me looking away. I tongue it; try to try to speak it, to speak it. But the thread only

keeps coming. Or maybe I never quite grasp the end of. And how to reflect on a thing of

which I can't quite conceive? No way to see the whole world all at once. So instead I

walk familiar circles through the day, a stylus carving corkscrews, calling them styles,

not far enough away to see the marks I've made. Never with a way to read the negative

space left in my wake. My course my only recourse. I am unthinking, two-dimensional,

except that sometimes the tiny wounds are even worse aren't they? The little bit of skin on the roof of your mouth that you can't help but tongue back and forth. Hardly even large enough to call a wound at all except that it won't go away. It stays sore and stays sore and stays though it's in the mouth where it ought to heal quickly. Except you can't stop, can't stop picking at the scab on your arm and old wounds become new wounds. And new wounds, just cut, they bleed so fast. Sliced by broken glass, shattered mirrors reflect the piecemeal nature of your wounded you. And cut a major vein, a bloodline without beginning or end, and you'll only bleed faster. But fast as you bleed you'll never catch up. No matter how fast you read the rosary in your head you'll never quite get around to the end or beginning. Some wounds don't heal. Some wounds are a dream that won't end. Some dreams are a life that won't end. But eternal life is no gift when there's only so much to be done in the world. Eventually you're bound to repeat yourself. And finally you find that even a stone is worn by the river that won't stop flowing but never moves from where it is. Movement that never gets anywhere. Eventually you're bound to repeat yourself. And how can you peel the bandages from a hurt like that? You can't. You can only wrap more bandages and more bandages and more. And anyway what good are bandages when the wound can't be touched? No good at all when it's only a fever that burns and burns and can't be healed except by burning out, burning up, burning down the structure that feeds it. Some wounds take only time, but time doesn't heal all wounds because sometimes there's not enough time every time. And you can put a leg in a cast, but not all wounds can be dressed. You can't put plaster on your pride. And who's to say that it's always about healing anyway? You might want to lick your own wounds, but you might as easily rub salt when you're someone else.

And some wounds just don't ever heal. Those are the ones that are only holes, empty

spaces. Nothing cut, nothing to sew back together again. Only lack, the wounds of

gaping void. Those are the wounds you can pack poultice into and slather salve onto but

they'll never be filled. And really you can do those things that won't work, but you

don't. You don't because those are the toothless holes that you dig into despite yourself.

Those are the wounds without bottom though you go looking. The bottomless empty is

the one that will only echo. No matter how many words you throw in, they'll only keep

falling in an endless string of letters. So many words thrown so fast for so long without

end that you forget what they meant, if they ever meant anything at all. But what else can

you do? How can a metaphysical wound be made tangible, touchable, something to hold

in your hands and even leave filled, fixed, finally fully understood and let go thanks to a

healing touch? It can't, at least not without exposing it, which leaves you vulnerable too

doesn't it? To infection, fester, decay, distort, derange, deny. Which doesn't sound very

good at all. Because all you wanted to do was share it, get a bit of you out of it. No,

expose you, rip the bandage back fast. But the strip is sticky and takes bits of skin with it

and the wound grows bigger. So you pick the strip up again and run it through your

fingers and read it carefully for those bits of skin you can pull free and piece together and

you think this way you'll make yourself whole again and cover the hole that caused the

problem in the first place, but the bits of skin aren't enough and only talk to themselves

and only fall down the hole that won't be filled and then you've got to dive down in after

because who knows where they're going or where they'll end up. If they'll ever end up

anywhere at all. And what once was merely a manageable wound has quite quickly

grown into a much bigger thing than you thought it was. And you look at the size of it

and think you couldn't possibly ever walk all the way round it and if you tried you'd walk so long that you'd come back around not sure if you'd finished or just begun. And you think that there's nothing worse than not knowing for sure and that's the problem with a problem that's really big isn't it isn't? And you think that you'd do anything to escape a wound so big as that and that nothing could be worse than that endless walk around the edge of it all. And that's the worst wound of all, the worst. Right? Right,

APPENDIX B[1]

---

[1] The editors, due to irreconcilable chronological, thematic, and sonic elements, have chosen not to include the following appended text - originally posted at The Archive on March 30, 2009 - in the Compendium. Despite its status as "other than" the novel in question and the resulting editorial disavowal, it has been here maintained due to its quantum existence as both potential sequel and possible prequel.

UP IN LIGHT

WE HAD TO TAKE A STEP, hold a pose, take a step, hold a pose, on and on like that to get anywhere. It was like pouring glass. Standing in someone's home like a misplaced garden statue, watching the dust settle, it was hard not to think about who might've lived there.

The dust was the reason we had to step so slowly. We didn't know then that it wasn't important to leave things as undisturbed as possible, and so we assumed that it was. Sealed inside our rigged up Hazmat suits, it was easy to feel only like an observer, not a participant, not an aggressor. With the radio turned down it was almost peaceful, eerie, but peaceful, like something from an artsy post-apocalyptic indie film, probably European. Of course the dust was too fine to be snow, though its dirty grey color matched the city slush we remembered from the old kind of winters almost exactly. The way it puffed up around even the most carefully placed foot, particles dissipating in the air, landing among a million parts per of their own, it could've been magical. Could've been if we didn't already know the dust consisted mostly of whoever had been standing there when everything went up in light.

That was what I thought of the first time I got to be the lead entry on a new site. I pushed the door open slow like they told me, like I'd seen so many times over past leads' shoulders. The view of the pristine room feeling me on my way in was intoxicating. It was desert wind on endless ash over loveseats and TV trays. Talk about defamiliarizing the home-sphere. I'd bought in wholeheartedly to the propaganda in the immediate after. I even took posters (we weren't supposed to) and put them up on the walls of my room. They should've just streamed a view of a room on first forensic contact. It would've worked on me. I was already there and it still worked on me.

We weren't all idealists though. There were some assholes who were in it for their egos. It's easy to be tough when everybody's already down to molecule omelettes. They took trophies, nothing major, but enough to pawn plus a few things to wear like scalps, since the scalps were always already gone before we got there - jewelry mostly, plus lots of watches. Which was stupid since none of them worked. I knew one guy who collected drivers' licenses. He flipped through them, all mangled and melted. He only kept the ones where the scans were still visible. Another guy collected car keys, which was, again, stupid since the cars were long gone. It basically made for annoyingly loud neckwear. They all just wanted something, something to make it worth it, something to keep the ghosts away by keeping them close. Who knows.

I did something sort of like it, though not for the same reasons I think. If anyone knew, and someone must have known, they probably figured I was the creepiest of the creepy. I just wanted a little bit, a little bit of each of them. Someone had to remember them, right? I know it was ridiculous. It's not like I could've done anything with it, even if I'd known how to do anything with it. If there was any DNA left in the dust, it probably looked about as human as a recipe for quiche. But I don't know, I wanted to remember, even if my remembering meant mostly imagining.

And I did imagine. I imagined I heard them all. They whisper when the dust brushes the air. They whisper when we finally sweep it all clean. They whisper that they're not gone. I can't ignore that. I have all those whispers, all those faded voices. I've kept them all in small plastic pouches, labeled and safe. I'm mapping the city that way. I've got a friend working on harvesting some old hard drives I picked up too. I'm sure I can find an IP directory, a utility record, something. They all had names before. Someone had to imagine them into existence once. I can do it again.

Maybe that's the real reason I do this. It's not "For Love of State." It's remembering the bones. It's painting over the bleached white skeletons, remembering our humanity, if we ever had any, or imagining it up if we didn't. Who am I to bring them all back? Nobody really, but I don't see anyone else caring.

I still remember the first time I saw the city as a kid. I'd never taken the tram so far before. I held onto my dad with one hand and leaned against the window with the other. It was huge. I thought it was alive. It sort of was, then. My dad must've seen the look on my face, reflected maybe in the glass. He lifted me up for a better view out and below. He clutched me to his front. I planted one foot on his thigh and one on the invisible glass.

"You see that?" he said. "That's what we're capable of."

We don't use the trams anymore, though I bet someone could get them working if they wanted to. Instead we do our slow stepping into the city, a million statues spreading out like time-lapse photography. Most days I try to start early so I can catch the sunrise over what's left of it. Every day when it comes into view I hear my dad's voice again in my head, another whisper I'm keeping in a labeled plastic pouch, pinned to a map of what was.

WORKS CITED

Althusser, Louis. "Ideology and Ideological State Apparatuses." *Literary Theory: An Anthology*. Ed. Julie Rivkin and Michael Ryan. Malden: Blackwell Publishing, 2004. 693-702. Print.

Archive, The. N.p. 1999. Web.

Baker, Nicholson. *The Anthologist*. New York: Simon & Schuster, 2010. Print.

Bal, Mieke. *Narratology*. Trans. Christine van Boheemen. Toronto: University of Toronto Press, 1985. Print.

Barnes, Julian. *Flaubert's Parrot*. New York: Vintage Books, 1990. Print.

Barthes, Roland. *S/Z*. Trans. Richard Miller. New York: Farrar, Straus Giroux, 1974. Print.

Baudrillard, Jean. *Simulacra and Simulation*. Trans. Sheila Faria Glaser. Ann Arbor: The University of Michigan Press, 1994. Print.

Benengeli, Cid Hamet. *The Ingenious Gentleman Don Quixote of La Mancha*. Trans. Miguel de Cervantes Saavedra. New York: Echo, an imprint of HarperCollins, 2005. Print.

Calvino, Italo. *Six Memos for the Next Millennium*. Cambridge: Harvard University Press, 1988. Print.

Caplan, Arthur. "Deleting Memories." MIT Technology Review. 18, Jun. 2003. Web.

Derrida, Jacques. *Archive Fever*. Trans. Eric Prenowitz. Chicago: University of

Chicago Press, 1995. Print.

Dickens, Charles. *The Mystery of* . Oxford: Oxford University Press, 1972. Print.

Dismembrance: A Strange Encyclopedia. Venice: Tokyo Kitchen Press, 2007. Print.

Dismembrance. Buenos Aires: Editorial Sur, 1942. Print.

Dismembrance. Minneapolis: Coffee House Press, 2009. Print.

Dismembrance. Pacific Ocean: Trident Books, 2014. Print.

Dismembrance. Dir. Shane Carruth. ERBP, 2016. Film.

Dismembrance. Tuscaloosa: FC2, 2001. Print.

Federman, Raymond. *Critifiction: Postmodern Essays*. Albany: State University of New York Press, 1993. Print.

Gale, Lucy M. *Discolorance: Remembering What's Missing in Dismembrance*. Venice: What Books Press, 2006. Print.

Gass, William H. *Fiction & the Figures of Life*. Boston: Nonpareil Books, 1971. Print.

Krause, Daniel T. "The Centrality of Marginality: Critical Apparatuses and Critical Figures in Creative Contexts." Salt Lake City: Tokyo Kitchen Press, 2013. Print.

Martone, Michael. *The Blue Guide to Indiana*. Tallahassee: FC2, 2001. Print.

Maso, Carole. *The Art Lover*. San Francisco: North Point Press, 1990. Print.

Mellville, Herman. *Moby Dick*. New York: Penguin Books, 1992. Print.

Moore, Alan. *Dismembrance*. Burbank: DC Comics, 2015. Print.

Shadow of the Waxwing. N.p. 1999. Web.

Shklovsky, Viktor. "Art as Technique." *Literary Theory: An Anthology*. Ed. Julie Rivkin and Michael Ryan. Malden: Blackwell Publishing, 2004. 15-21. Print.

Sorrentino, Gilbert. *Mulligan Stew*. New York: Grove Press, 1979. Print.

Sparrow, J.R. *Sacred and also Profane: Reading Dismembrance*. Salt Lake City: Kannon Books, 2005. Print.

Shandy, Tristram. Volume X. New York: W.W. Norton & Co., 2014. Print.

Tokyo Kitchen Press. "The Mahabharata." Tokyo Kitchen Press, 2014. Print.

Vander Wal, Thomas. *Reading Dismembrance: Taxonomy of An Audience*. Sebastopol: O'Reilly Media, 2012. Print.

INDEXES

METAPHORS

Asemia, Ambrose, Amygdaloid, Animalia, Anonymiad, And if tracing is a device meant for nothing more than enabling the novel's action, then it is nothing less than the fulcrum by which the earth is moved. And if the heart does nothing more than pump the blood that moves us, who would argue that the heart is a part of the body but not the body?

Art is a way of experiencing the artfulness of an object: the object is not important.

Art creates a vision of the object instead of serving as a means of knowing it.

Art is not a form of simple communication.

Barth, Barthes, Barthelme,

Caudate Nucleus, c'est moi

D—

E— in the room.

Featherman, Foster Wallace, Fatalist,

Gravity's,

Hyperthymesia, Historiographic, Holes, tied with string

Jeu, Jacques

K

Lorem Ipsum dolor sid hamet

Mulligan Stew, Memorelliana, Michael, Minotaur, Mobius, Musashi

No shell,

On a winter's night, if

Or it becomes the telling of the telling of the telling of the telling of a story.

Plateaus...
.... 1000

Piglet, greased

Quixotic

Re—

Spindles, Mirrors

Tattoo, Tokyo Kitchen Press

Un—, Up In Light, Ungulate

Verification, Veracity, Versions

When she woke in the mourning, she found the typewriter infested with ants. The irony did not escape her. Nobody was making typewriters anymore.

X, the spot

You might as well start from dreaming and work your way back from there. The jars were always already empty anyway.

Zero

MURMURATION

AND AFTER ALL THIS I haven't found you still.
We came in by different doors.
To resect sounds
Like a return, a
Coming together, a
Rendezvous, a reunion
But means to cut out.
And intersect sounds
Like meeting but
Means to divide by
Passing through or
Lying across.
A touch that breaks
Apart.
That's how th s works.
And feel hands on   i   me
Now.   won't find .   I

                              me   your
-from *Di mbrance*   you y
                       I   our
      me   me   w   e
                she you her them   i
         i   he we   him us   we
      him   they I   it   they   me   theywe
      She we you   we *me*   Iyou   we he
         us   me I   wemeyoushe
              you   I   theme she
              he we   h   i   m
              her   you
                             her
                             they

139

theywemeheyouIyoutheysheyou   wehemeweshetheyusyoumeweyoumeIhetheyi
usheshweusyouhewemeyou   herhehismehimwetheysheImeweheyouIwehe
wetheyhemeussheweusme   usyoumewehetheyIamweusmeshehetheywhous
hemeweshetheyweusmeyou   weshehetheyusImewhymeusyouthemweshehethey
weshehetheymeweusthey   youImeweheshetheyusyouusyouusmeweheshetheyI
Iwemyweusyoutheyshe   wemeheshetheyusyouImewewhotheyusyoumeweshe
youmeIwehesheusthemus   meyouuswehetheyshetheywemeustheyuswetheywhoI

we youtheyweIshetheyhe herhishimweus theywemeuswe you themusmehimwe
shewehemeyou they   I methemusshemehe youmewe Iyouwe Iweshethey
heshehe   meweyouweyouwe ustheyhemesheheweshelmemy
we   metheyweshemehe theyus you wemethey
    meyouuswehetheyshetheywethey   she
    youtheyweIshetheyhe Ishethey   wethey
    sheweusushetheywemeshe   meyouthey
    shehetheyweyouImeweheus   theysheweyou
    wemeheus himherustheyme   themyoumeIshewe
    shethemuswehimsheuswe   Ishe   usmeI
   us wetheyyoumemywehe   you   she
   herhishimweus youmyuswehe   they   I
   usweheshelmemy uswe he themthey   she
you she me Iwetheyheus I theyshe they we he meyou
   us theysheyoume shewethey usyouhe   he   they
   theyweme uswe theyyoushewehehe   she   ushe   I
we you they us we us youtheyyou   he   you   us
   she she we you us I me we we   you   mehe   she
   you us they SheHe we they   they   we   meyou
   mewememe they I she wethey   she I   ustheyhe
weyou i us   you youwethey   himmeusshel
they me she they us we ushe   Imeweyouhesheus
us the we I you she we they me   usmeyouhimmeweshe
it we you me I we us they us you   theywesheusIme usmeus
us the we shethey   Iwehe   usyoumewehe   sheI
we you us me I   they mewe   weme   we
Iyou the we   him   he   theyweus   they
me them   she I he
they   her   she   weme
   us   heme   us
him   we   they
   we   theyshe   me
     they   sheheshe
     me

usmehimwesheitheytheyuswemey
mehimwesheittheyussheheitwesheusous
himwesheitthey   wemewesheyou
wesheheitus   mewethey
youmeshe   weus
meshe   you
we   I
me   me

                           we
      uswethey
yousheheweusmeherwe   they
sheheweusmeherweyoushe weusthey   he she
heweusmeherwesheyouthemme   she
weusmeherwesheyouthemweusthey   you   they
usmeherwesheyouthemweustheysheher   we
meherwesheyouthemmeuswesheImeweyou
herwesheyouthemmeuswesheImeweyoumewe   I
wesheyoutheymewehesheusmeImeweyoumewe
      they   theyme   me   I
        we   you   we me u   he
          me   we   she   she
youmeusweshe usmeyou   I   me
meusweshehe   shemeweme   I   we
ustheyweshemeusyoutheyyuswe   me   you
wemesheyouItheyyuswehetheymewe   you   I
shemeyouuswetheyheImewe   me   I
meuswesheusmeyou me   I   I
uswesheheusmewethey   I   I
wesheheusme   weshe   I   I
sheheusmewethey   they   I   I
heusmewethey heshe   us   I   you
     me theyhewe   me   I
        shethey   I   I
        useme   I
        them   I
          we   I
          I   I
          I   we

DANIEL TAKESHI KRAUSE'S work has appeared in two languages, three countries, and four dimensions. His work has been performed or printed most recently in *Hairstreak Butterfly Review*, *Dream Pop Journal*; *Halophyte*; *Versal*; at the Banff Center in Alberta, Canada; in *A Bad Penny Review*; and *Sugar House Review*. He completed his PhD in English at the University of Utah. He currently lives in Newport Beach, CA.

WHAT
BOOKS
PRESS

LOS ANGELES

CPSIA information can be obtained
at www.ICGtesting.com
Printed in the USA
LVHW090609091120
671134LV00024B/325